CLEAN SLATE

A SINS OF THE MAFIA WORLD NOVEL

SCARRED HEROES BOOK 3

GWYN MCNAMEE

Clean Slate
© 2022 Gwyn McNamee & Christy Anderson

This book is a work of fiction. Names, characters, establishments, or organizations, and incidents are either products of the author's imagination or are used fictitiously to give a sense of authenticity. Any resemblance to actual persons, living or dead, events, or locales is entirely coincidental

PROLOGUE

MOUTH

The crosshairs at the center of my scope remain frustratingly empty, our target either not there or not presenting himself.

Yet.

Though it's been almost twelve hours of sitting, watching, waiting for the prime opportunity to take out my mark, I continue to remain vigilant because he *will* make an appearance.

They always do, eventually.

Even the most well-trained adversary on the battlefield makes a mistake. And the current target is far from that.

He's nothing more than a selfish, entitled prick who thinks he can get away with doing whatever he wants to women by virtue of his wealth and power over the politicians who control making him pay for his crimes.

And John Blaire is definitely someone who needs to pay.

Even if that means waiting here 'til the sun comes up and coming back again and again until the right moment presents itself to find final justice for his victim...or victims—because there's no way a guy like this only does *that* once.

Joanie was just the first one who had the guts and determination to come forward to try to press charges. The system may have failed her, but we won't.

I won't.

Reaper nudges me with his knee from where he sits beside me, with his back to the high roof wall of the building a few streets over from our mark's condo I use as a perch. "Anything?"

I shake my head. He releases a long sigh and glances at his watch, which seems to be moving agonizingly slowly this evening. We won't have much more time dawn. Once it does, we'll need to hightail it out of here.

Fewer prying eyes at night. Fewer chances someone sees something that can get us caught. If I can't seal the deal before the sun comes up, I'll come back tomorrow and do this all over again.

Reaper peeks over the wall toward Blaine's building and huffs back into his spot. "Either this fucker somehow slipped out of his condo without us knowing, or he's been in his bedroom with that redhead for close to twelve hours." He shakes his head and laughs. "I wish I had that kind of stamina."

I snort and chuckle.

Don't we all...

The government may have trained us to be machines in the game of war, but those skills don't automatically equate to being machines in the bedroom.

Reaper grins and waggles his dark eyebrows. "Though, Vik isn't complaining."

I roll my eyes at him, then return my focus to the dark condo lined up in my scope. After the way Chaos and I saw Reaper going at Vik in the shower when they were holed up in the safehouse in New York, I wouldn't imagine she *would* have anything to complain about. Reaper is good at everything he does—including his woman. Apparently, a lot.

If only I could say the same.

It's been so long for me that I likely forgot how to do it altogether.

Just like I forgot everything else important.

A low buzzing draws my attention away from the scope for a moment, and Reaper reaches into his pocket, pulls out his phone, and checks the screen, wincing slightly before bringing it to his ear. "Parrish, didn't think I'd be hearing from you anytime soon."

Me, either.

The last time our paths crossed in New York, it was a bloodbath that almost ended very badly, and a call from Parrish out of the blue can't be a good sign. Getting involved with the Satan's Knights MC again isn't high on my to-do list, but the former club president wouldn't be reaching out to Reaper if it weren't important. That doesn't bode well for us.

Reaper listens to the other end of the line for a moment, his jaw tightening. "You're fucking kidding me."

That doesn't sound good.

I return my focus to the quiet, dark condo several streets away while Reaper deals with whatever cluster-fuck Parrish has gotten into this time.

"Where is he now?...Uh, huh...Fuck...We'll take care of it...Yes, I'm sure. Obviously, time is of the essence."

Definitely not good.

He releases an annoyed groan, shifting positions beside me. "I'm tied up on a job here, and Chaos has some personal shit going on at the moment and won't be available for a few days, but I'll send Mouth."

I jerk my head toward him, furrowing my brow and mouthing, *"What the fuck, man?"*

Is he fucking kidding?

The last thing I want to be doing is heading back to NYC alone to handle something Parrish needs help with. The Knights may have been allies in our mission to take down the Yankovich organization and stop the human trafficking ring they were running, but they aren't people I want to start doing regular favors for.

Reaper gives me an "*I'll explain later*" look. "Yeah, no problem. It'll be done by the end of the week." He ends the call and shoves his hand through his hair, tipping back his head to stare at the sky above him, the stars barely visible with the light pollution D.C. produces. "Those fuckers in New York..."

I raise an eyebrow.

He drops his head to the side, meeting my gaze, and nods. "Yeah, *those* fuckers...the Russians who were selling women off a fucking menu like rare wines...turns out we didn't do as good of a job cleaning away that stain on humanity as we thought. One of the Yankovich cousins stepped in and picked up right where they left off."

Fucking hell.

That family is full of evil douchebags. They seem to just keep coming out of the damn woodwork.

I scowl at Reaper's information, then return my full attention to our mark. After sitting here for so long, I don't want to miss the moment when it presents itself.

"That was Parrish. He said this asshole, Maksim Yankovich, came over from Russia shortly after the warehouse raid to help clean up the mess we left, and they've been keeping an eye on him. They already started getting wind of a new auction taking place next month. Those fuckers...just when you thought you wiped some major scum off the face of the planet, more of it pops up."

He shifts to face me fully, and I peek at him out of the corner of my eye, tension building at the base of my skull, waiting for what he's about to say.

"I know you're worried about going alone, Mouth, but I need to finish this job for Joanie. After we take care of Blaine, we still have two more to take out, and as soon as Chaos is back, I'm going to need him on that with me." He pauses for a moment, and even though I keep my focus on the still, dark condo in the scope, I can feel his eyes on me, boring into me and assessing me the way only Reaper can. "You can handle this."

Easy for him to say.

He isn't the one living in this head, this body, dealing with what I do, day in and day out. I'm not the person I was when we were in Delta. And he seems to keep either forgetting or ignoring that. He has more confidence in me than I have in myself.

What we did in New York was a good step in the right direction. It proved there are still *some* things my brain hasn't forgotten, those ingrained reflexes and habitual movements that still make me lethal. Working with the guys since then has kept me busy, kept me moving, and kept me from dwelling on all the things I lost, but to try to pretend it will ever be the same as it was before *that* day would be lying to myself. This is just the way it is now, the way it will always be. And Reaper needs to accept that I'm not the same man I was.

I keep looking through the scope, so he won't see the way his comment affected me. His hand falls on my shoulder. Despite trying not to, I flinch at the contact.

He squeezes firmly, the move somehow familiar, bringing bits of a hazy, distant memory. "You can do this, Mouth. Maybe it's exactly what you need to get back in the game."

I haven't been in the game for so long that I don't even know if I remember how to play.

At least, it sure feels that way.

An op on my own.

No one watching my back.

Chaos and Reaper have both done it—gone out on their own and completed missions for clients and friends. But they don't have the *complications* I have to deal with. They have their shit together. They've both moved on from everything that happened, despite the scars they'll always carry. Somehow, they've found a way to live with the constant reminders of what we all lost in order to concentrate on something real that's right now.

Maybe it's time I try to do the same.

If that's even possible.

Reaper shifts next to me, wincing slightly, his body likely stiff from sitting on this hard roof against a brick wall for the entire night. "It should be a relatively easy in and out. The guy has settled in Brighton Beach, in one of the other warehouses owned by Nikolai Yankovich, and after what happened to his cousin, he's tightened security. It would be a problem for anyone else, but not you.

"Parrish is going to have his crew stake him out until you can get there to help figure out when and where's the best place to hit him. All you have to do is pull the trigger and get back here." He pauses for a moment, like he's considering his words. "No matter how you may *feel*, you're still the best shot of anyone I've ever met, Mouth. I trust you to have my back. Always. And I trust you with this."

I trust you to have my back...

A lot of people have. Some regretted that decision.

I close my eyes, trying to picture their faces, but all I get are brief flashes that I can't connect with any names or places. It's all one big jumble, a complicated mess of memories, dreams, and nightmares that will never straighten out.

Going to New York alone is a risk. But it's one I have to take. If I don't, a lot of innocent people are going to get hurt.

That auction next month needs stock for the menu, and that means they'll be collecting them soon. The faster I can get to Brighton Beach and take out the fucker running things now, the greater chance we'll have at stopping the trafficking business before they are at full speed and it's too late for a group of girls.

I glance at Reaper and give a quick nod, letting him know I'm in.

A slow grin spreads across his face, and he squeezes my shoulder again. "Good. Now, let's hope this fucker comes up for air soon so we can get this over with and go home."

A-fucking-men.

After two weeks of stalking these three fuckers, following them and watching, determining the best time and place to take out each of them, neither of us expected to have to sit this long, waiting for the opportunity at Blaine at his own place.

He really does have stamina.

Lying in this position for this long used to be nothing for me. I could go an entire day, even longer, without moving a fucking muscle, but now, a dull ache starts to form at my temples and the base of my skull. I clench my teeth, trying to will away the migraine before it starts to get bad.

Not now.

Not tonight.

I can't afford to have that interfere with my job. Joanie deserves this relief, this form of justice.

A light flickers on in the window of Blaine's condo, and I ready myself, shaking off the pain to concentrate on the here and now and what's important.

Reaper glances up and over the roofline. "Thank God he came up for air."

I chuckle and wait, but the condo remains quiet. No movement. Whatever Blaine is doing with that redhead we saw him bring home earlier, it's certainly keeping him occupied.

She finally appears, her breasts scarcely contained in a tiny tank top, booty hanging out of barely-there shorts. The girl wanders into the kitchen and opens the fridge, leaning into it, giving me an excellent view of her tight ass.

There was a time I would have made a smartass quip about it, and the guys would have all laughed. At least, I *think* that's what used to happen. Chaos and Reaper say it was, and I have no reason to distrust them after everything that's happened since that fateful night. Occasionally, one of those comments even still pops up in my head, sitting right on the tip of my tongue, but now, I bite it back.

I have to.

The redhead pulls out a bottle of orange juice from the fridge and drinks straight from the carton.

Fucking gross.

Her hotness level just dropped by about five points, but then again, she's with Blaine—apparently voluntarily—so that brings her down to a one. The girl needs to be more careful and selective about who she gets involved with.

She places the juice back inside and reaches for something else.

Come on, Blaine. Get your ass out of that bed.

The man we've been waiting for appears stark naked from the bedroom to the left, seemingly unconcerned with the entire wall of floor-to-ceiling windows that share everything with the world—or at least anyone bothering to look.

Like me.

He makes his way over to her as I dial in the scope, perfectly lining up the shot.

Dead calm.

No wind.

Five hundred ten meters.

Not that long ago, this shot would have been a given. One I could do in my sleep, with one hand tied behind my back. But now, even after the years I've spent rekindling the ingrained training, trying to awaken those instincts and natural reflexes, I have to take a deep, calming breath to get my heart to steady and prevent my hands from shaking.

You got this.

One shot.

Clean.

Blaine approaches the redhead, wraps his arms

around her, then presses his lips to the side of her neck. She backs into him, rubbing her ass against his crotch.

Oh, God.

If I have to watch these two fuck before I can take him out, this is going to be a really long night.

Blaine reaches around her, grabs a container of strawberries and a bottle of what looks like champagne, and turns toward the bedroom.

So, he is a rapist and a romantic...

I snort to myself.

This lowlife thought he got away with what he and his buddies did that night. He believed he could walk away from the horror they enacted against Joanie and pretend it never happened. And maybe he could have, if not for one fatal mistake—they left her alive.

The criminal justice system may have failed her by not being able to convict these guys—but that's where we come in. And after all the evidence we've seen against them, no amount of money or connections will save them from our brand of justice.

He releases the redhead, laughing, and turns back toward the bedroom. One. Two. Three. He finally steps far enough away from the woman for me to pull the trigger.

The shot hits him square in the chest. He drops instantly, the champagne bottle shattering on the floor, bubbling up across the smooth surface.

I can't hear the girl scream from here, but she jerks around, her hands over her mouth. Blaine doesn't move as blood pools under him.

A heart shot.

He was dead before he even hit the floor.

Content that he's not getting back up, I sit back and turn to disassemble the rifle and police my brass.

Reaper grabs the casing before I can and holds it up. "That was quite a shot. Now, go do the same fucking thing in Brighton Beach."

I'll certainly try.

1

FINLEY

The buzz of conversations around me mixes with the steady bass of the 80s classic rock song, filling the trendiest new speakeasy-themed bar in New York, Keys and Heels, with an upbeat, welcoming atmosphere—at least for most of the patrons.

I take a sip of my gin and tonic and watch the blond supermodel in the booth across the bar with Schwartz. Whatever he just said to her shifted her entire body language toward him. This isn't going to end well for him, and I'm just waiting to enjoy the fireworks.

Whenever David Schwartz is involved, there always seems to be some.

Sometimes—like tonight—I have to remind myself that he's a brilliant lawyer who can teach me a lot; otherwise, I might quit and walk out the door to hang up my own shingle when his bullshit hits the fan. Which it looks like will be any second now...

A large body steps in front of me, blocking my view of the free entertainment. "Hey, is this seat taken?"

I let my gaze drift up the man, over his dark jeans, black polo shirt, and to his striking green eyes and dark, ruffled hair. He motions to the open spot beside me on the couch.

"Looks like it's not."

He grins at me and slides onto the cushion, intentionally pushing his thigh against my bare one. I roll my eyes and shift away from him an inch. I was willing to give him an opportunity to take his shot, but he isn't exactly starting off on a good foot.

The chances of my bringing him home for some fun tonight just went down significantly with that suave move.

"So"—he leans in closer to me—"what's your name?"

For a split second, I consider giving him a fake one, but the entire reason I came out tonight was to blow off some steam and maybe find someone to help me release a little tension. So, I shouldn't brush him off completely without giving him a second chance.

"Finley," I answer without looking at him, instead focusing on the full-on argument now happening between Schwartz and the model. "Finley Banks."

I take a sip of my drink as the model throws hers in Schwartz's face. That almost makes me choke, and I chuckle against the rim of my glass.

The man next to me follows my line of sight. "What's so funny?"

"See that guy over there?" I motion toward the booth near the bar. "The one with what looks like an entire drink dripping down his face…"

"Yeah?"

"Well, that's my boss. Kind of."

I may have to listen to Schwartz day-to-day on certain aspects of my practice since he signs my paychecks, but it's easier not to think of him as my boss when I made the mistake of sleeping with him while I was a law student.

"Damn, looks like he's not having a very good night." The man on the couch with me shifts closer, brushing my leg again with his, and his palm comes down on my thigh. "But *you* can."

Oh, hell no.

I slowly turn my head toward him and lock our gazes. "I highly suggest you remove your hand from my thigh before I break it."

His eyes widen slightly, only instead of removing the offending appendage, the asshole grins and squeezes my flesh. "Oh, you like to play rough. I can get into that."

"The only thing you'll be getting *into* is a police car or an ambulance if you don't take your hand off me right now."

"Whoa, lady." He jerks his grubby mitt off me and opens his mouth to argue. "You—"

I push to my feet, not missing the way his eyes zero in on my exposed legs and heels, even after my warning.

"Let me give you a piece of unsolicited, free legal advice. Not only do women *not* want to be treated like pieces of meat but touching one like that is third-degree sexual abuse under the laws of the State of New York."

He gapes at me. "What are you, an attorney or something?"

I snort and down the rest of my drink in one gulp. "Or something."

Apparently, my doctorate doesn't prevent me from being nothing more than a potential lay for a perv like this asshole. It shouldn't be surprising, but I had hoped tonight I could meet a nice guy and enjoy myself without being smashed in the face by misogyny.

I turn away from him without another word and make my way over to the booth where Schwartz sits, wiping the drink from his face with tiny bar napkins, the model nowhere in sight.

Fighting back a grin, I slide into the side of the booth she just vacated, setting my empty glass in front of me. He looks over at me and releases an exasperated sigh. I can't stop the laugh this time, shaking my head and pointing at his empty tumbler on the table that likely once held a single malt scotch—his usual drink.

"Looks like you could use another."

He glowers at me. "It's not very becoming to revel in the misery of others."

"Not reveling." I motion for the waiter and point to our empty glasses while Schwartz tosses the dirty napkins onto the table. I lean forward, returning my attention to him, fighting back a smile. "Swear, I'm not reveling."

"Yes, you are." He bites the inside of his cheek, the tiniest of grins playing at his lips. "You're taking pleasure in my misery. It's all over your pretty little face."

Pretty little face...

It's crap like that from Schwartz that makes working with him so frustrating sometimes. He respects the hell out of what I do in a courtroom for our clients, but he just can't seem to rein in the inappropriate comments that cross the line more often than not. That's partly my fault for ever letting him get in my pants. But when you're a young law student and a handsome, successful attorney flirts with you—especially when you've had a few strong drinks—you don't think about the fact that you may end up working with or *for* the man later in your career and have to look him in the eye with the knowledge of what his junk looks like.

As per usual, I ignore the sexist remark he likely thinks is world-class flirting. Inappropriate shit from men is just part of the job when working as a trial lawyer, and David Schwartz is no different. I understood it before I ever went to law school, and nothing has changed despite years of building up my reputation.

"What did you say to her that pissed her off so much?"

He offers a shrug. "Nothing too offensive."

I tip back my head and laugh, the sound eaten up by the din of the patrons filling the almost-impossible-to-get-into bar. "I know you well enough to know that isn't true."

He scowls at me and reclines against the booth seat, stretching his arms across the back of it. "Okay, so maybe I pissed her off, but that's only because she has a problem with honesty. Throwing her drink at me—that was a bit extreme."

Cocking my head to the side, I dart my tongue across my lower lip, considering how great it would feel to do the same to him sometimes. "I might have thrown a drink at you for some of the things you've said to me if I had one handy."

That grin of his makes another appearance, and he lowers his arms and leans in too close for professional comfort. "Yet you still went to bed with me."

The waiter has perfect timing, appearing with our drinks and setting them in front of us.

"Thanks." I immediately take a sip of mine, and as soon as the waiter retreats, I point at Schwartz. "That was once—a long time ago. I was very young. Very drunk. And very horny. It's not going to happen again."

He shrugs and grins at me mischievously. "I can try to wear you down."

"I would advise against it."

One of his dark eyebrows rises. "Offering your boss legal advice, are you? That's cute."

"Seems like you need it."

He chuckles and reaches for his drink, but as his fingers close around the glass, the shrill ring of his phone cuts through the tension between us. A quick glance at the name on the screen brings a litany of curses from his mouth. He swipes his finger across the screen and brings it to his ear.

I sip my drink and watch him, waiting for him to flip out on whoever seems to be annoying him so much.

"You've got the worst fucking timing, Parrish, and for that, my rate just doubled." Schwartz practically hisses his words into the line, and given who is on the other end, I can't blame him.

His relationship with Parrish and the Satan's Knights has always been complicated, to say the least. After being saddled with representing the club when his father moved to California to run the West Coast office of their firm, it's a weight I'm sure he'd love to have off his shoulders. They always seem to be getting into some kind of trouble Schwartz doesn't want to be dealing with.

Schwartz's hand tightens on the phone. "An associate? I don't run for your pals, Parrish." He listens to whatever the former president of the ruthless MC says on the other end and snarls. "Where are you?" He pulls the phone away from his ear and swipes the screen before bringing the phone back to his ear. "I'll be right there."

He slides out of the booth with an annoyed groan.

"Where are you rushing off to?"

He slips his phone into his pocket and pulls out his wallet. "That was Parrish." He drops some bills onto the table. "One of his associates got locked up." He points toward his untouched drink. "Help yourself to that when you're finished with yours."

I smile at him, despite the annoyance I still harbor toward the man. This is just how it is with David Schwartz and how it likely always will be. "I just might. See you tomorrow."

Schwartz makes his way out of the bar, and I lean back in the booth with a sigh, scanning the room for anyone else interesting even though I'll more than likely just head home alone.

It's been a long fucking day already, and dealing with douche canoe over on the couch just made it feel even longer. But at least I'm not stuck going to one of the jails tonight like Schwartz.

That really would put a damper on the evening.

MOUTH

REAPER WAS RIGHT. After what we did to Yankovich's organization the last time we were in New York, they're ready for us—or whoever else they might think could be coming for them. They've closed ranks and increased their security tenfold over what they had at their various locations only months ago.

More men.

More cameras.

Less risk for them.

They think that will keep them safe, but they've underestimated me and what I'm capable of—or at least, what I *was* capable of and *hopefully* still am.

The ache at my temples starts up again, and I lower myself to the roof and roll onto my back, squeezing my eyes closed against the pain that has become almost a constant over the last few years, especially in stressful situations.

It will dissipate with time.

It will get better.

The empty promises made to me over and over again ring in my head, slamming against my skull in a beat that only seems to be racing toward an agonizing crescendo.

Better. Yeah, fucking right.

I was stupid to believe the doctors when I knew in my heart it never would get better, and I was stupid to think I could somehow come to New York and take care of this mission without it interfering. But Reaper is counting on me to get this job done, and the women these fuckers are dragging into their web of sex and violence need to be protected.

There isn't any time for weakness. Over the years, I've pushed through worse, kept working, kept firing, kept others alive even when I was bleeding, exhausted, and on my last fucking leg.

I can do it again. I have to.

It seems like I've gotten here in time to stop another auction from happening since the girls don't appear to be here yet, but I need to act quickly. The longer this guy has to make plans and try to get the organization back up and running at full speed again, the greater the chance innocent women are going to get hurt.

Get in the game, Mouth.

I shake off the cloudiness fogging my brain, push away the pain, and flip back onto my stomach to return to my perch and watch my prey. With so many other things I can't remember clearly, this—stalking and waiting—feels more natural than anything else I do daily.

This was my life. This is what I did—hunted and protected my men. Yet so much of it is lost. The good and the bad. Some of the memories are better left in the past, though. Too much pain lies there, too many mistakes and consequences. Those are the ones I dread, the ones I hope never do come back fully. The flashes I get of them are enough for me to know I don't want them to ever become crystal clear.

And I won't make a mistake tonight.

I can't.

The weapon in my hand has always been my best friend, the tool I relied on over and over again to do its job as long as I did mine. It's a part of me. Still, tonight, I'd much rather be handling this guy up close and personal.

A nice knife to the gut and genitals. A little water-boarding to really send a message. Maybe even some sleep deprivation. There are just so many things I'd love to do to him to make him really pay for his actions. But New York City has too many eyes. There's always somebody watching or a camera recording. Always someone with the potential to see something you don't want them to, and I definitely don't want any witnesses for this.

The moment that fucker makes a mistake, he's mine. No amount of security will protect him from the bullet with his name on it. Justice will be served, one way or another.

He's been good, though. Meticulous. Not even stepping outside to get into the car, only entering through a covered, protected garage at his place or inside the warehouse.

This is a man who's aware that what he's doing has made him a target. He's paranoid for a reason. Likely after he discovered what happened to his cousin here, he knew he would be up against an opponent he couldn't eliminate first.

All this careful planning and protection will be for naught, though.

Everybody fucks up, eventually. Everybody gets complacent. It's what people in my position count on to get the job done, and I will get the job done—hopefully, tonight.

Not that I don't enjoy a nice evening in Brighton Beach, but it would be a lot better without this migraine and *with* a little bloodshed.

And my opportunity may be finally presenting itself.

The rear door to the warehouse he's been operating out of swings open, and one of his men steps out, an unlit cigarette dangling from his mouth. It's his routine. Every thirty minutes, almost to the second. And each time, he props open the door, giving me brief glances of movement inside.

All I need is for the right man to take the wrong step.

Maksim Yankovich's goon pulls a Zippo from his pocket and lights his cigarette, sucking on it like it's oxygen. The irony almost makes me chuckle, but I hold it in and keep my eyes on him and the open door.

Several sets of feet walk past, but nothing else is visible. Nothing that will give me certainty of my target.

It's a waiting game—and *this* game, I can play.

Almost like the big man upstairs is giving me a giant *fuck you*, the migraine roars back, stronger than before, a piercing pain that makes me wince and grit my teeth.

Not now.

Not now.

Not now.

The smoker glances over his shoulder at someone and yells something I can't make out from here. I wait a moment for something, anything, to happen. The flash of movement behind him might have been missed by someone else, someone without my keen eye and experience, but all it takes is that split second for Maksim to step toward the door to respond.

Crack.

Crack.

I fire off two rounds, taking out him and his man standing outside almost instantaneously. They both crumble to the ground, dead before they even hit it.

Mission accomplished.

But there isn't any time to enjoy my success.

Even out here, surrounded by dilapidated buildings and warehouses, there are eyes and ears. Someone will have heard those shots even if it takes a few minutes from Yankovich's men to process what happened, and I need to be long gone before anyone starts searching for where it came from.

I pack up my rifle, grab the shell casings, and start to push to my feet. By the time anyone can come looking for the source of the shots, I'll be blocks away, strolling down the street toward where I parked my getaway car like nothing even happened.

In theory.

As soon as I get halfway vertical, the world spins around me like I'm stuck on some sadistic merry-go-round. I clamp my eyes closed against the agony assaulting my head. My stomach turns, vertigo and pain making acid crawl up my throat.

Fuck.

This one is bad—perhaps the worst I've had in months. And history tells me it's only going to get worse —fast. There isn't any way I'm going to make my exit plan.

Time for plan B.

All I have to do is keep my shit together long enough to get to the basement of this shithole.

I stagger over to the door on the roof that leads to the stairwell and step through it, kicking away the rock I had holding it open to let the door slam closed behind me. Staring down at the four flights of stairs, the world tilts, and I have to swallow back the bile, my vertigo kicking in even stronger.

There's no time for weakness, Mouth.

Complete the mission.

Do what must be done.

I stumble down the steps as fast as my unsteady feet will carry me, but the wail of police sirens hits my ears, and I freeze.

Fuck.

A squad must have been in the vicinity and heard the shots. There's no way those assholes called this in. The last thing Yankovich's men want are the cops crawling around that warehouse.

I double-time it the rest of the way into the dark, dank, dilapidated basement; the only thing keeping me vertical is my iron grip on the handrail. A quick scan of the dark space ensures I'm still alone. Even though this warehouse has been empty and condemned for years, vagrants still use it as a flop house at times. It's currently visitor free.

Thank fuck.

The last thing I need is a witness. Getting out of here without being caught will be hard enough as it is when I'm like this.

I make my way to the far corner to the spot I found during my first surveillance of this place, pull my rifle out of the soft case, and break it down quickly with trembling hands.

My vision shifts in and out of focus, and I reach up to the foot-wide hole near the top of the brick wall and drop each piece into the gap between the ancient foundation and the earth behind it, one by one.

Each part clanks ominously, and I fold the rifle case and shove it as deep down into the hole as I can.

No one will find anything here. Once the smoke clears, one of the Knights or I can come back to get everything. It will require pulling down more of the wall to access it, but so be it. That's a problem for later. Right now, I need to focus on getting the fuck out of here.

The sirens grow louder as I stagger toward the stairwell, head twisted in an invisible vise.

Feet thud against the concrete above me.

Fuck.

I scan the basement, knowing what I'm going to find. The only window is far too small for me to get through. There's only one way out, and that's back up the stairs and through the main warehouse, without whoever is up there seeing me.

Unlikely to be a problem if I were at the top of my game, but I'm far from that at the moment. My stomach roils, and I hustle up the steps, gritting my teeth against the stabbing in my head, then pause at the top and listen for signs of anyone else.

It's quiet. A little too quiet since I know someone just came in. Maybe I'm lucky and it's a vagrant and not a fucking cop or one of Maksim's men who somehow followed the shot.

Easing my way out and along the wall, I keep to the darkest of the shadows, away from the faint moonlight coming in through the broken windows on the opposing wall.

One of the exits is only a few feet ahead.

So close, I can almost smell freedom.

Get there, Mouth.

A blinding light hits my eyes. "You there, freeze! Police!"

Fuck.

I throw up my hands against the harsh beam made ten times worse by the light sensitivity I always suffer during one of these attacks.

My night just turned into a clusterfuck, and it's about to get worse.

I can't fight the nausea anymore, the flashlight in my eyes and the hurried movements finally getting the better of me. Despite my best efforts to choke it back, I turn to the side and wretch, the contents of my stomach splattering against the cracked concrete at my feet as the officer advances with his gun drawn on me.

Fuck.

2

_____

FINLEY

The shrill ring of my cell phone wakes me from what was about to be a fabulous dream. Strong muscles. Warm skin. Expert hands. All of it was about to culminate in something I had hoped to find earlier tonight.

Instead of the payoff, I groan and roll onto my side, fumbling on my nightstand until my hand finally wraps around the offending device.

I pull the screen toward my face, squinting against the brightness. "Fucking Schwartz..."

There are only two reasons he'd be calling at two a.m. Neither of them is good.

I accept the call and bring the phone to my ear. "I told you at the bar that it's not happening again. Go to bed, Schwartz."

"Not a booty call, Fin. I wish I was calling for that, but you need to wake up."

His tone makes my brain fully snap awake. I push myself into a seated position and scrub my hand over my face. "Why? What's going on?"

"I need you to head out to Brighton Beach. 60th precinct."

"What? Now?" I double-check the time on my clock. "It's two o'clock."

"I know, but I'm still dealing with the issue Parrish called me about earlier tonight over on Staten Island, and now, two more of his associates got picked up in Brighton Beach."

"Fuck...doing what?"

"I'm not entirely sure. You need to go see both of them and make sure neither of them talks. Figure out what you can before they get in front of the judge."

"This can't wait a few more hours?"

If these guys are Parrish's "associates," they should know not to talk, and I can grab a bit more sleep before I have to drag my ass all the way out to Brighton Beach.

"No. One of them is Wolf's son."

"Shit..." I scrub my hand over my face, trying to wake myself up. "I'm on my way. Text me the info."

I throw off the covers, end the call, quickly grab appropriate jail clothes from my closet, and toss them onto the bed.

It's far too late—or too early—to be doing this, but when the son of the president of the Knights gets popped, going immediately isn't even a question. Wolf isn't the kind of man you mess with, and you don't keep his son waiting in lock up.

I step out into the kitchen and punch the start button on the Keurig to get a cup going while I change and haphazardly pull my disheveled hair back into a ponytail, so it doesn't look like I just rolled out of bed—even though I did.

Typically, I'd never let a client see me with bags under my eyes and looking haggard as hell, but I'm too tired to care and Schwartz will kill me if I make Wolf's son—and whoever this other client is—wait any longer than necessary.

Only the blackest of coffee will help me right now. I grab the travel mug, pop on the top, and head out the door with my briefcase in hand. Between the drive out there and these meetings, by the time I'm done, I'll have to come straight home and shower before heading to court for my morning calendar.

What the hell is going on tonight?

Three of Parrish's guys all picked up at almost the same time?

I unlock and open my car door, glancing up at the full moon.

That explains it.

That and the fact that anyone associated with Parrish always ends up with at least one foot in shit at some point.

The only thing that keeps me awake during the half-hour drive from Staten Island to Brighton Beach is chugging the black coffee and wincing at how bitter it is. I'd much rather have a triple latte, and God knows I'll be getting one as soon as I leave the damn police station. But at two in the damn morning, I can't be picky about where I get my caffeine.

It's just the glamorous life of a criminal defense attorney working for Schwartz.

I pull up in front of the 60th precinct building, park, and make my way inside, feeling slightly more awake than I did forty minutes ago. Locating my identification, I approach the front desk sergeant.

He glances up at me over the top of his wire-rimmed glasses. "Can I help you?"

"Yes, I'm attorney Finley Banks, and I need to see two people you have in custody."

The bored-looking man glances at his watch. "It's two thirty in the morning, ma'am."

"A fact of which I'm intimately aware, sir, but that doesn't change my needing to see my clients immediately."

He releases a deep sigh and flips through a stack of papers on a clipboard in front of him. "Their names?"

I scan the text Schwartz sent me after we hung up. "Vincenzo Scotto and...Jude Lawson."

Another annoyed sigh slips from his lips. "I don't have a Jude Lawson."

"Then, he's likely listed as John Doe."

The man stares at me for a moment, his hard eyes narrowing, then scans his paperwork again. "First-degree murder. Two counts. Nice."

I fight a wince.

Of course, it has to be a murder case in the middle of the fucking night.

"Which one would you like to see first, ma'am?"

"That depends. Are either of them currently in questioning with detectives?"

The corner of his mouth quirks up into a little half grin. "I'm not sure, ma'am. Likely not Mr. Lawson since he hasn't said a single word since they brought him in. Wouldn't even give us his name."

Not a single word?

Smart criminals know to keep their mouths shut, but most at least ask for their lawyer or a phone call. Hell, a *bathroom*. Something.

"Let's start with Mr. Scotto, then."

"Ah, a first-degree assault charge. Starting out light."

I scowl at him. At this hour, I could do without the sarcasm. "Buzz me through. I know the way to the meeting room."

He shoves a clipboard at me to sign in, gives my ID a cursory glance, and presses the button under his desk to unlock the door that will get me into the precinct. I make my way down the hall toward the meeting rooms and slide into the first one with an open door.

Pulling out my legal pad and pen, I cover a massive yawn with my hand.

So much for the black coffee.

Hopefully, these meetings will be quick, and I can get home for at least a nap before I have to make myself presentable for court.

Heavy footsteps make their way down the hallway

toward me, and a uniformed officer leads in my first client. Dark eyes meet mine from beneath tousled brown hair. The scruff covering his jaw can't hide the way he clenches it as he glances back at the officer escorting him, who pushes him down into the chair facing me.

"Thank you, Officer." I look down at the cuffs on his hands. "Please uncuff him."

The officer gives me an exasperated look. "Ma'am, that's against policy."

"I don't care. Uncuff him. I need him to be able to write."

"He can write just fine with cuffs on." He turns and closes the door behind him, effectively ending that debate.

The young man stares at me from across the table, his knuckles swollen and bloody.

"Vincenzo Scotto?"

He nods. "Call me Enzo."

"I'm Finley Banks. I'm an attorney, and I work with David Schwartz. Parrish and your father asked for me to come to see you to figure out what's going on."

He relaxes slightly.

"They arrested you on first-degree assault charges, and from the looks of your hands and the spot of blood on your shirt, it seems to me they might have a case. So, tell me what happened."

Enzo lowers his head, taking in the speck of blood, then looks back at me. "My stepbrother owns a boxing gym, and I nicked myself shaving."

Smartass.

But he's just trying to protect himself. I can't really blame him for that.

"Whatever you tell me must remain strictly confidential. Protected by attorney-client privilege. You're going to go before the judge in the next forty-eight hours. We're going to face whatever these charges are, and it's helpful to know what we're up against so we can get in front of it."

He reaches up and rubs his eyes with his palms, a task made all the more difficult by the fact that they're still cuffed together. "Brent Matthews donates to my father's charity, Frankie's House. He was holding a fundraiser tonight in Staten Island. I thought I'd show my support."

I quirk an eyebrow at his casual clothes. Jeans and a T-shirt are hardly appropriate attire for a fundraiser. "Dressed like that?"

He shrugs. "I wasn't aware of a dress code until I arrived at the place. That's why I didn't go in. I was about to leave when I saw Danica, Brent's ex-wife, step outside. She and I are...well, we're acquainted."

I purse my lips. "Acquainted?"

He shakes his head. "It's not like that between us. Look, when she walked outside, she was with Matthews. They were arguing, and when they left, I suspected something bad might happen. I followed her to make sure she was safe. They came out here to Brighton Beach. She confronted him; they started yelling at each other, then he grabbed her. I got out of my car and intervened."

"Badly enough to charge you with a first-degree assault." Which means Mr. Scotto did some serious damage to the man who is currently running for office.

"You and I both know Brent Matthews is a powerful guy. He's running for Congress. But everyone has skeletons in their closet. They put on a good front, but their marriage didn't end simply because they grew apart. He's been treating her like shit for a long time. Now, I witnessed a heated argument between a divorced couple, and the second he raised his hands to her, I separated them. He took a swing at me, and I defended myself."

"Are there any witnesses? Anyone who might be able to back up your story?"

Convincing the DA that a prospective congressman is an abusive asshole is an uphill battle. We'll need to dig deep and find some evidence to support Mr. Scotto's allegations if we have any chance at defending this.

Enzo stares at me for a moment, contemplating his response before he nods. "Brent's ex-wife will back me."

"Are you sure she'll tell the same story?"

"Yes."

"All right. Well, that's good." I jot down a few notes. "You'll go in front of the judge tomorrow or the next day. The charges will be read, and they're going to set a bond. I'm sure your father will get it posted as soon as possible. They'll set a preliminary hearing date, but given that you were arrested on the scene, have a couple of busted-up knuckles, and have blood on your clothes, we will likely want to waive that hearing and gain access to the police reports and any other evidence quicker. This will come down to what his ex-wife says and whether the DA believes you and her or the alleged victim." Not a slam dunk by any means when the man is in a position like Brent Matthews. "Do you have any questions right now?"

"No. I'm good."

"Okay. Then, sit tight. Keep your mouth shut and head down." Things I'm sure his father and the Knights have taught him over the years. "I'll see you at court."

I push up from the table, make my way to the door, and open it. The officer stands just outside and glances over at me with an annoyed look. He doesn't want to be doing this at three in the morning any more than I do.

"Finished with Mr. Scotto. Can you please bring in my next client?"

His jaw hardens. "Ma'am, he's here on a double murder charge."

I raise my eyebrows at him. "Your point?"

"We typically wouldn't allow anyone to meet with him without additional security measures."

"*Anyone*?" I cross my arms over my chest. "Or a woman?"

He freezes for a second, then opens his mouth and closes it again, likely second-guessing what his response would have been when he sees the glare I'm giving him.

"Go get him."

Muttering something about blood-sucking lawyers, he steps in and grabs Mr. Scotto, jerking him to his feet a little too forcefully. I offer him a parting smile, and they make their way down the hallway toward the holding cells again.

Misogynist asshole.

I return to my seat to jot down a few more notes about what Enzo just told me. If it's true—that he witnessed an assault and was intervening—this may be, at worst, a defense-of-others claim. The complication is the victim's position—something we'll definitely have to address once we get the written statements and other evidence.

Footsteps sound down the hallway again, and I wait for John Doe, aka Jude Lawson, who apparently, has been arrested for two murders, to be brought in.

Lovely.

The officer appears in the open door with my new client, dressed head to toe in jail garb.

I don't know what I was expecting, but it sure as hell wasn't this.

Icy-blue eyes cold enough to freeze anything they look at assess me with an intelligence I rarely see in my clients.

No fear.

No panic.

No sense of unease.

Despite sitting in here on these very serious charges.

Instead, a heat simmers beneath their surface. A danger contained only through sheer will and confidence.

My misogynist friend leads him in and seats Mr. Lawson across from me, holding up a hand. "Don't even bother asking about the cuffs." He stares at Lawson for a moment, then turns his focus to me.

"Good luck. This guy hasn't said a single word since he was picked up."

"Then how did my firm find out he was in custody?"

The officer smirks. "He had a notebook in his back pocket. We pulled it out while we were stripping him. He pointed to it, and the detective gave it to him. He wrote 'phone call' and a number on it. The detective dialed it, and this guy wrote, 'Tell him where I am,' and that was the end of that. Whoever was on the other end hung up and then, I assume...called *you*." He narrows his eyes and shakes his head. "All very strange."

Indeed. Maybe Mr. Lawson is deaf or mute?

He moves to the door and pauses before closing it behind him. "Thanks for giving us his name, though. Helpful since his prints haven't brought up anything."

No record?

That's definitely unusual for one of Parrish's guys. Most of them have a rap sheet a mile long and the attitudes to match it. But this guy...

Broad shoulders. Lean, hard muscles visible under the jail clothing given to him. Eyes that seem to see right through me while they also strip me bare. A calm that makes me more uneasy than anything any client has ever said to me before.

Jude Lawson stares back without reaction to me or anything the uniformed officer said.

The door clicks closed, and I take that as my cue to jump right in.

"I'm Finley Banks. I'm an attorney. I was sent here by Parrish to represent you." I pause to try to gauge his reaction and to attempt to determine if he can even hear me. "I'm happy to hear you haven't said anything potentially incriminating." I offer him a half-grin, but all that earns me is more continued staring. "They have you here on some pretty serious charges."

He doesn't react, just continues to analyze me with the cool gaze that somehow heats my body all the same, his large, muscular body immobile.

I shift on my hard, plastic chair to try to dispel some of the strange sensations of having him look at me like that sends through me. "I already know you didn't say anything to the arresting officers or detectives. I need to make sure you can hear me and understand what's happening, Mr. Lawson."

MOUTH

Ms. Banks' frustration rolls off her like a tidal wave set on destroying whatever she thinks it is that keeps me from answering her.

Stupid. Stubborn. Arrogant. This woman likely believes all of these things about me.

And why shouldn't she?

To her, I'm just another criminal who got busted, who forced her to roll out of bed in the middle of the night to come down here and hold his hand. Another in a long line of clients who don't respect her or what she does and only see her for what she is on the outside—a stunning woman who could just as easily be on the cover of a magazine as in a courtroom.

No doubt, she's used to having chauvinistic men—like the officer who just led me in here and even her own clients—give her shit because she's a beautiful woman doing a job they despise and think should be left only to men. Her days are likely spent dealing with that type of asshole, the kind who make her prove over and over again that she belongs and that she can win her cases in heels bigger than their dicks.

I don't envy her at all.

Every man I ever served with had to prove they belonged there—me included. Each one of us was put through the wringer. We were the best of the best. And something tells me Ms. Banks is one fucking fantastic attorney.

Parrish wouldn't trust her to represent someone if she weren't, and her entire energy has filled the room since the moment I was brought in. It bounces off the tight walls, a "don't try me" vibe emanating from her in a way that can't be denied.

She may be tiny, but she doesn't back down. And all she wants is my cooperation. The least I can do is confirm I understand what's happening.

I offer the tiniest shift in my head, just enough to let her know I'm listening.

"Good, I'm glad you're with me, but I need to know what they said to you and what, if any, physical evidence they may have before we go into the arraignment so I can start developing our plan of attack."

I remain still, assessing the woman sent by the Knights to help me.

Frustration tightens her grip on her pen. "Mr. Lawson, I don't think you're quite grasping the seriousness of this situation here. I understand not speaking to the police, but not speaking with your lawyer is going to cause a lot of problems. I can't do anything for you if you won't talk to me. I'm here to *help* you, but you need to help *me* first."

She keeps her clenched hand around the pen poised on an empty sheet of paper that she likely had anticipated being filled with notes by now.

Her green eyes bore into me, not looking away for even a second.

Impressive.

She's the first person in a long time who has been able to stare me down and not be intimidated. This tiny, five-foot-nothing woman who can't weigh more than a buck-twenty has more balls than some of the men I've served with.

Ms. Banks must be an absolute shark in the courtroom.

Thank fuck she's on my side rather than at the prosecutor's table.

I'm going to need someone like her. Someone who doesn't back down from anything. The cops may not have found the weapon, but they have enough to hold me and charge me.

Not only was I caught trespassing in a condemned building, but they also have a vagrant who heard the shot while on the street below only minutes before. Seeing them speaking with him outside when they perp walked me made me want to puke again.

The only thing saving me from assured conviction is this woman and the fact that New York's finest don't have the resources to tear apart a three-story dilapidated building to conduct an in-depth search for the rifle. They'll do a cursory search, at best, perhaps assume I had someone else with me who got away with it, and hopefully, they'll leave it at that.

But even if they may not be able to convict me in the end, they can make my life hell while the charges are pending. Ms. Banks will surely do her best to ensure that doesn't happen, but she'll have to do it without my help.

"Mr. Lawson?" She raises a thin brow at me, tapping her pen against the legal pad.

The tick, tick, tick might be annoying to someone else. Not me. It's almost...therapeutic. Like a metronome clicking back and forth, setting a steady tempo. All the tension in my head eases for a brief moment concentrating on the sound.

A brief flash of a memory flutters through my mind.

Broken images...

A woman at a piano.

The ticking of a metronome.

Music filling the room.

Warmth and comfort.

A feeling of being home.

Secure.

Safe.

"Mr. Lawson, please." Her tension seems to have ratcheted even tighter while I've been lost in the shattered memory. "Help *me* help *you*."

Despite the continued pain in my head, I fight the twitch of my lips wanting to smirk at that phrase. So many people have said it to me over the last few years—my team, my doctors, the government, others who claimed to care. Yet they all disappeared when it was clear I wasn't getting better and would never remember why I should care about them and that I would never be who I was before that night.

Help me help you...

People say the words in an effort to get you to let down your guard. But some guards are in place for a very good reason. Those words rang in my ears, said too many times to count by too many people who should have been able to make it better.

A lot of good it did.

I'm not any better now than I was when I woke up after the explosion four years ago. If anything, the migraines are only getting worse, the memories fuzzier as time passes rather than coalescing and coming back the way I was promised.

The longer it goes on, the more confusing they become until I can barely tell what's real and what's a dream or nightmare anymore. That, coupled with the almost daily pain, becomes unbearable at times—like earlier tonight. The only thing pushing me forward is my mission, the jobs Reaper, Chaos, and I do. The justice we seek for people who can't get it anywhere else.

I just need to keep reminding myself of that when I feel like I do now.

At least I haven't puked again.

Doing that in front of a beautiful woman like this would be...embarrassing. It's bad enough having to sit here across from her in jail garb while she's in a form-fitting suit that accentuates her curves. Even the slight bags under her eyes she didn't bother to try to hide can't mar her true beauty.

It shines in her eyes—along with her determination and irritation.

She's a good person, just trying to do her job. And while I'd like to help her, the headache throbs behind my eyes, radiating out through my whole head. The only thing that will end it is a day of sleep or my meds, which I'm not getting to anytime soon, apparently.

Ms. Banks sighs and sits back in her chair, flipping the pen between her fingers and staring at me for what feels like an hour, waiting for me to break.

She has no idea who she's dealing with. Men far stronger and—maybe—more determined than her have done far worse things to get me to talk...and failed.

I cross my arms over my chest and wait, my eyes locked on her green ones. Something flashes deep inside them, something that, for a moment, almost makes me open my mouth to answer her questions. But I know what that brings, so I bite back the words like I do every day of my life.

Finally, she throws up her hands and shakes her head. "All right, Mr. Lawson. I guess I'll do the talking, then. If you have something to say, you let me know. If you don't want to talk, I'll give you my notepad and pen."

She sighs. "In the next forty-eight hours, you'll be led out of here to the courtroom. You'll appear in front of the judge, who's going to look at a criminal complaint the district attorney's office is drafting right now. That complaint is going to charge you, more than likely, with two counts of first-degree murder and any other charges they can throw at you because I can tell you right now, Mr. Lawson, they'll do everything they can to keep you in custody. And the more charges they can pile up, the less likely you are to be able to meet the bond that gets set. If you're stuck here, that puts them at an incredible advantage preparing for trial."

She taps her pen against the table, letting her words sink in.

"It makes it very hard for me to argue on your behalf when you won't talk to me, when I have no idea who you are, why you were there, what you were doing, or have any explanation I can offer the court that would give the judge a reason to release you on a reasonable bond while we try to figure this thing out." She leans forward slightly, the top of her breasts just barely visible in the V-neck blouse she wears under her suit jacket. "I'm on your side, Mr. Lawson. It would behoove you to start acting like it."

Her words are meant to terrify me, and with her typical clients, her tough attitude and no-nonsense approach probably scares them into complying with her requests. It probably makes her job easier when clients know they can't walk all over her just because of her appearance. In her profession, looking like a cover model probably makes it harder for her to get people to take her seriously. She's fixed that by becoming an unbreakable pillar of strength and determination.

If they let women on Delta Force, she'd have been a real badass operative.

Exasperation finally getting the better of her, she shoves to her feet and practically throws her notepad and pen into her bag, her eyes still on me. "I'll see you in court soon, Mr. Lawson. And I seriously want you to consider your attitude toward me. This type of behavior isn't going to get you anywhere."

She stalks past me, her thigh lightly brushing my shoulder. Despite layers of clothing between us, a little buzz of electricity courses through my arm and radiates into my entire body. I swallow thickly, listening to the click of her heels on the linoleum until I hear the doorknob twist in her small hand.

Something burns in my chest, something I haven't felt in so long. I don't even recognize it. And it has nothing to do with the permanent brain damage that has ruined my life. It's because I haven't experienced it before, at least, not that I can remember.

For some reason, for the first time I *can* remember, I actually *care* what someone thinks about me. I actually care what *she* thinks about me. I don't want her believing I'm a total asshole who's being difficult and uncooperative just because I can be. I want her to know I appreciate her being here, coming down in the middle of the night to ensure I'm taken care of and protected. I want her to understand this has nothing to do with *her*.

I want her to know the *truth*.

No matter how painful it may be to admit it to her.

Slowly, I turn my head to the side, swallowing to give myself a moment to get my tongue and mouth working when I haven't used them to speak for so damn long. "Th-th-thank y-y-you, M-M-Ms. Banks."

Out of the corner of my eye, I watch her freeze, her hand still on the half-open door. The fingers wrapped around her briefcase ease their grip slightly, and she looks over her shoulder at me, her green eyes meeting mine without blinking.

There it is...

The familiar look of pity.

The thing I've been avoiding during this entire conversation.

The look I knew would come as soon as I opened my mouth.

No one sees me the same after they know. Even those who know who I am and what I'm capable of no longer see me as an elite military operative. All they see is someone to feel sorry for, someone who needs their sympathy. They see a weak mind when really, it's just this stupid fucking body that betrays me.

But unlike most people I deal with, the look of pity vanishes from her warm gaze just as quickly as it appeared, and her perfect pink lips curl into a kind smile.

She inclines her head to me, acknowledging my

statement, then walks out and leaves me sitting in the room by myself to consider what just happened with my new attorney.

Well, that went well.

It certainly wasn't what I was expecting when they told me my attorney was here. *She* wasn't what I was expecting. I never could have anticipated the way she would make me feel, the need to have her understand the thing I've kept hidden from so many for so long.

It definitely complicates things.

3

FINLEY

The judge steps out from his chambers and takes his seat, glancing at some paperwork on the bench before nodding to his clerk. Enzo shifts nervously beside me, and I reach out and squeeze his shoulder.

This isn't routine for him, and he has every reason to be nervous. Now that I've seen the damage he did to the alleged victim, I can see why the State is pushing these charges. You can't cause that kind of damage to someone as high profile as this and expect them to let it go.

The clerk pulls out a file from a stack on her desk and calls the case.

Judge Forest acknowledges us with a nod and accepts the file from her. "Appearances, please."

At the table next to me, the prosecutor clears his

throat. "The State of New York is represented by Jonathan Waters."

I smile at the judge. "Attorney Finley Banks appears on behalf of Mr. Scotto, who appears in person and in custody. Good morning, Your Honor."

"Good morning, Counselors. We're here for an arraignment. Mr. Waters?"

Waters flips open his file to read from it. "Your Honor, the defendant is charged with one count of assault in the first degree, in violation of New York Penal Code section 120.10." He rattles off the penalties and other required items for the arraignment before moving to the bond. "The state is asking for a $10,000 cash bond, Your Honor. Mr. Scotto assaulted a congressional candidate and beat him so severely that he may have to have reconstructive surgery on a shattered orbital socket. He was still present at the scene when the police arrived. This is a very violent crime, Your Honor. Mr. Scotto poses a danger to the community, and therefore, a substantive cash bond is warranted."

"Thank you, Mr. Waters." The judge raises a brow at me. "Ms. Banks?"

"Thank you, Your Honor. Mr. Scotto is twenty-eight years old, has lived in the greater New York City area for his entire life, and has not had any police contacts prior to this incident. He has not exhibited any sort of violent behavior or in any way demonstrated that he poses a threat to the community. The state paints a very rosy picture of the alleged victim in this case and the facts surrounding it that they believe support their version of events, but I can assure this court that Mr. Scotto in no way poses a danger to anyone. As the court is aware, the purpose of bond is to ensure compliance and appearance in court and to protect the public. Mr. Scotto has a full-time job, numerous connections to the community, and there is no reason to believe he won't make all court appearances and cooperate with his defense. Therefore, we are asking for a $5,000 cash bond."

The judge examines Enzo for a moment. "Mr. Scotto, these are very serious charges. You understand that?"

Enzo straightens his shoulders even more and nods. "I do, Your Honor."

"You understand that if you're released on bond, you must make all your court appearances and will not have any contact with the alleged victim or any of the witnesses in this case. If you do, that could result in additional felony charges?"

"Yes, Your Honor."

The judge hands the file to the clerk. "Given Mr. Scotto's ties to the community, his lack of prior record, and the statement of his attorney regarding his cooperation with her, I'm going to set a $5,000 cash bond. Standard conditions including no contact with victims or witnesses."

I nod at the judge. "Thank you, Your Honor."

The clerk quickly gets us a date for the next hearing, and I scribble it onto my calendar and start pulling out Mr. Lawson's file.

Enzo looks over at me, and I lean in. "You can go with

the officers. They'll have the paperwork. Your dad will have you bonded out quickly. Call me tomorrow."

He nods his understanding. "Thank you, Ms. Banks."

The courtroom officers approach and lead him back to the holding cell. No doubt the Knights will have him bonded out within an hour. My other client, I'm not so sure. I have no idea how this will go at all, especially given the information I've been able to gather since my meeting with the enigmatic Mr. Lawson.

They bring him into the courtroom, and he carries the same stoic look he did when I saw him in the meeting room in Brighton Beach, not giving away anything. But his eyes still rake over me with a heat that makes me shift uneasily.

There's just something about Jude Lawson that's impossible to pinpoint, and now that I know his history, it sheds a completely different light on our entire first meeting.

I offer him a tight smile as he takes the chair next to me, unwilling to do anything that might reveal how unsettled he makes me. As expected, Jude doesn't do or say anything to acknowledge me, where we are, or why we're here.

"The State of New York versus Jude Lawson..." I tune out the calling of the case, pulling out the criminal complaint and my notes for the bond argument.

The judge accepts the next file. "Appearances."

"The State of New York appears by Jonathan Waters."

"Attorney Finley Banks appearing on behalf of Mr. Lawson, who appears in person and in custody."

"Your Honor, the State has charged Mr. Lawson with two counts of murder in the first degree in violation of New York Penal Code section 125.27 with the anticipation that additional charges may be forthcoming as we continue to investigate. This was a brutal double homicide that took place in a populated area with what appears to have been a high-powered rifle. Mr. Lawson is the most dangerous threat to the community I can imagine, and therefore, we're asking for a $2 million cash bond."

Two million?

I glare at the prosecutor, hoping he'll feel my disdain for his request even if I can't voice it.

The judge raises an eyebrow. "Ms. Banks?"

"Thank you, Your Honor. Mr. Lawson is thirty-two years old, was born in Canton, Ohio, to a father who was career army and a mother who was a homemaker. Both are sadly now deceased. He has two younger sisters and served honorably in the US Armed Forces, enlisting when he was only eighteen years old and remaining on active duty until he was medically discharged about four years ago. Mr. Lawson has not had a *single* contact with law enforcement in his entire life."

I pause to let my words sink in, glancing between the judge and prosecutor but intentionally avoiding looking at Jude. Not when I can feel his eyes locked on me instead of where they should be—the judge.

He's wondering where I got all this information since he didn't give me anything the other night. I thought I was going to have to go into this without any ammunition to argue for bail, but thankfully, Parrish came through with what I needed. Though, something tells me that having this knowledge is only going to make things more tense with Jude.

If he had wanted me to know any of it, he would have told me—or at least written it down.

The man wanted me in the dark about his background and medical situation. I won't speculate on why, but now that I know, his tension rolls off him palpably.

"Let me repeat that, Your Honor. I'm not talking about an arrest or conviction. I'm talking about not a *single* police *contact*, not a *parking ticket*, not a *speeding ticket*. Nothing. Mr. Lawson served his country and has respected the laws of this country his entire life. Mr. Lawson is exactly the type of law-abiding citizen we expect everyone to be. Whatever the State thinks happened here, Mr. Lawson is not a threat to this community. He's a protector of this community, which he showed in his exemplary military service. There is no reason to believe he will not be cooperative with me or make his appearances in court. I would ask the court to set a reasonable $10,000 cash bond."

Judge Forest directs his attention to the prosecution table. "Mr. Waters, any response?"

"Your Honor, Mr. Lawson does not have any contacts we could find in the city of New York or the state of New York. As far as I can tell, his employer is in Baltimore, Maryland, where he resides, and given his military training, the state has serious concerns about Mr. Lawson disappearing should he be released on bond."

I shake my head. "Your Honor, may I respond?"

"Yes, Counsel."

Here goes nothing.

If Jude was uncomfortable with what I told the court before, he's really not going to like this.

"Your Honor, Mr. Lawson suffered a major traumatic brain injury in an incident overseas four years ago. Due to this injury, he now deals with debilitating migraines, memory loss, as well as a speech impediment caused by the brain damage."

Jude's hand tenses into a fist on his thigh under the table, and I reach and lay mine over his to keep him from doing something stupid in court. He tenses slightly at my touch, but I squeeze gently and brush my thumb over his, trying to comfort him somehow when he clearly doesn't want this information out in the world—or for me to know it at all.

"He's dependent on multiple medications to treat this brain injury, none of which were available to him during his time in holding. Mr. Lawson is not in any position to be fleeing the country, nor does he have any reason not to appear before this court, given the weak nature of the probable cause in this case. The State has no weapon. Their evidence is loose and circumstantial, at best."

I pull my hand away from his, returning it to the top of the table, but still feeling his skin under mine. Swallowing thickly, I glance at the prosecutor before focusing on the judge again, trying to ignore the heat still radiating through my body at the innocent contact.

"Mr. Lawson's employer *is* in Baltimore, but if the

court should require it, Mr. Lawson can and does have a place to reside within the state of New York while the charges are pending. And he would be more than happy to do so."

MOUTH

I LOOK OVER AT HER, watching her mouth move and hearing the words coming out of it but not really understanding or processing them, still feeling her touch lingering on my hand and through my chest.

How the hell does she know all this?

And what the hell is she talking about, a place to live in New York?

That migraine that hit me the night I took out that Russian scum was a brutal one, but I think I would have remembered telling her all that background information...and having a damn place in the city. Which I most *certainly* don't.

While the judge considers his notes, she glances over at me and offers me a half-smile, not giving away anything. If her little squeeze of my hand affected her the way it did me, she's doing a damn good job of concealing it.

Finally, the judge sighs and leans back in his chair, looking at me with a shrewd gaze. "Here's what I'm going to do, Counsel. While I appreciate your client's service to this country and understand your position concerning his medical status, these are very serious charges with very serious consequences. And while I agree that probable cause may be light in this matter"—he tosses a look to the prosecutor—"it *is* there, nonetheless. If it weren't, I'd be entertaining a motion to dismiss. Which means, I have to take into consideration the protection of the public from Mr. Lawson and what he's charged with. Therefore, I'm going to order a $500,000 cash bond along with electronic ankle monitoring. And I'm going to require that he turn over his passport and remain in the state of New York while these charges are pending."

Ms. Banks nods, trying to bite back a smile at her victory. "Understood, Your Honor."

She climbs to her feet while I'm still working on trying to figure out where she got all this information, what the hell she was talking about, and the feeling her touch sent through me.

An officer steps behind me and uses my cuffed hands to pull me up, gripping me a little too tightly. I don't even acknowledge him, just wait for directions either from him or Ms. Banks.

I could have him on his back and end his life in ten seconds, even with my hands cuffed, but it doesn't do me any good to fight with this guy in the courtroom, even if he's clearly looking for one.

My determined and apparently sneaky-as-hell lawyer leans over to me. "I spoke with Reaper last night. Your bond will be paid—most likely today. I'll pick you up and get you set up at an apartment Reaper rented for you."

Well, hell...

I haven't given her nearly enough credit. She must have put the screws to Parrish and insisted he connect her with someone who could give her some information on me. Either she got Reaper's number, or he called her. She wasn't going to let my silence prevent her from doing her job and representing me the best she could.

Fucking brilliant.

It shouldn't surprise me at all that she managed to pull this off, given the way she stood up to me the other night and failed to be fazed by my silence.

I incline my head toward her, acknowledging her work and thanking her in the only way I can, and she smiles and reaches out to squeeze my shoulder. Her hand remains there a second longer than it should, and something passes between us that makes a shiver run through me despite the heat in the courtroom.

Her pupils dilate slightly. She shakes her head and jerks her hand back like she's been burned, then grabs her briefcase and hustles out of the courtroom while I get led in the opposite direction, still feeling her touch on my arm.

Even three hours later, when I push open the door from the jail and walk out onto the dark New York City street to find her leaning against a BMW, scrolling through her phone, I can still feel that heat.

The rush.

The energy that passed in that simple action.

This woman is dangerous.

And not just in the courtroom.

The jail door slams shut behind me, and her head jerks up, her green eyes finding me quickly.

She pushes off the car, wearing skin-tight jeans and a loose top that hangs off one shoulder, exposing her collarbone. "Oh, hi." Shoving her phone into her pocket, she scans the street on either side of us, avoiding looking at me as her cheeks redden. "Sorry that took so long. When you're dealing with that much money, the clerk's office sometimes takes forever crossing their *T*s and dotting their *I*s."

So confident in our meeting and the courtroom earlier today, now she seems frazzled.

By what?

Having to leave me there for the rest of the day before I got bailed out?

I offer her a shrug to let her know it's no skin off my back. Really, I could have stayed in there forever and not given much of a shit as long as they could get my meds. I can sleep just about anywhere and block out the noise under normal circumstances. This migraine is finally tapering off naturally after a few days, but who knows what the next one could bring. Being unprepared never ends well.

As I've just proven.

Not that I didn't plan this mission. I did, down to the fucking last second from the moment I left Baltimore to what was supposed to be my return trip home. But I can't predict when my body will betray me anymore. Which is why I had plan B—the damn hole in the basement wall. At least being caught without the weapon makes their case almost impossible to prove beyond a reasonable doubt.

But my weakness is what got me caught.

It was exactly why I didn't want to come to do this alone and why I didn't want to talk to Ms. Banks when she was trying so damn hard to help me the other night.

Now, she knows it all, and it's going to change everything, the entire way she sees me and this case.

She shifts awkwardly on her feet, now clad in Chucks instead of the four-inch stilettos she sported during our jail visit and court this morning, and motions toward her car. "Um, I'll take you to your new apartment. The Knights got it set up for you with some basics—clothes, food, etcetera."

How kind of them...

She steps around the front of the car and slides into the driver's seat while I open my door and take the passenger seat. Almost instantly, her scent invades my lungs—crisp, minty, citrusy—and my cock stirs.

Fucking hell.

The stank of the jail and the musty smell of the courthouse masked this before. I shift awkwardly in the seat while reaching for the belt to relieve some of the tension building below mine. She glances over at me furtively, starts the car, and pulls away from the curb into the light evening traffic.

I rest one hand on my thigh and massage my temple with the other, an almost constant motion for the last few days.

The longer we're in the small car together, heading

away from the jail and toward wherever I've been set up to stay, the more her scent permeates my every breath, making it harder and harder to sit still. I turn away slightly, staring out the window, watching the dark streets blur by, cracking the window in a vain attempt to get some fresh air instead of smelling *her*.

Normally, during a migraine, watching this would make me lose my stomach again, but...

But it's completely gone.

At some point during this awkward, tense car ride, my migraine completely disappeared.

Impossible.

That never happens. It slowly dissipates on its own most of the time, but without medication, it could take a whole damn week, and there are times I have to go to the neurologist for emergency treatment when it gets really bad.

Yet, somehow, in a matter of minutes, all traces of the headache that has been plaguing me for days have vanished.

I sit up straight, letting my hand fall away from my temple, and glance over at her, but she keeps her eyes on the road in front of her, seemingly unaware of my confusion—or maybe intentionally ignoring it the way I've been trying to ignore the pull I have toward this woman.

We reach a red light, and she finally feels my gaze on her and looks my way.

One of her eyebrows wings up. "Are you okay? You look...confused."

Shit.

The last thing I need is her knowing how she affects me. She has one job—get me off.

Of the charges.

The charges ONLY.

She narrows her eyes on me, concern furrowing her soft brow. "Do you need something? Something I can get for you on our way to your place?"

Nothing you can buy at a store.

The light changes to green, and she sighs and relaxes back in her seat, her focus returned to the road. Her hands tighten and twist on the wheel, the tension building in her body.

Finally, she glances my way again. "Look, I understand we don't know each other and why you might not want to have a friendly chat, but I'm trying to—"

"H-h-help me. I kn-know."

She flinches, and I instantly regret my words. I didn't mean them to come out sounding so...angry and annoyed. But tone is definitely hard to convey when you can't get words out without stuttering.

Shit.

I scrub my hands over my face and sigh. "S-s-sorry."

She shakes her head, forcing a half-smile. "You don't have to apologize, Mr. Lawson. You've had a rough few days. Your friend, Reaper, he sent some medications he said you need. Said you likely left them somewhere you can't get back to them right now."

Like the damn glove compartment of the car that has long since been towed by now and is sitting in some impound lot.

It isn't her fault I fucked it all up, and I'm going to

need her to get out of this mess. If that's even possible. So, the last thing I want to do is have her pissed off at me or thinking I'm mad at her for just trying to help.

"Th-th-thanks. I really d-do appreciate it."

She swallows thickly, something clearly running through her head that she's struggling with voicing. "I'll do whatever I can to help you, Mr. Lawson. Please, just trust me."

That's easier said than done, but I sure as hell don't have anyone else here I can.

"P-p-please, call me Mouth."

Her head jerks in my direction, her lips twisted. "Mouth?"

"It's a l-l-long story…"

One I am in absolutely no position to tell—nor would I want to even if I were capable of it, especially to a woman who stirs up so many things inside me.

Lust.

Need.

Hate.

Concern.

Rage.

I didn't know one person could bring them all, yet somehow, she has.

And that's a very dangerous thing for a man in my position.

4

FINLEY

No matter how hard I try to concentrate on the stacks of discovery spread out across my desk, my eyes keep drifting to my computer screen and the headline in bold spread out across the e-version of the *New York Post*.

PURPORTED RUSSIAN MOB LEADER KILLED

Shit.

The last thing Mouth or I need is the local news latching onto his case and turning it into some sort of exposé on organized crime violence in the city. While I can't say I shed a tear over Yankovich or his man's deaths, that doesn't mean I want a spotlight on the fact that my client *may* or may *not* have been the one to take them out of commission.

I certainly don't want to be spending my time fielding calls from reporters when I have a trial coming up in a month on the Bergman case, motion hearings on three others next week, and need to get Rick on investigating both Mouth and Enzo's cases and securing statements from anyone and everyone who can help in either.

A sharp knock on the door jerks me from my trance, and Terri grins at me.

"Sorry, didn't mean to scare you." She holds up a big, brown paper bag. "Ho Wop just delivered your lunch."

Thank God.

It's an excuse to get away from this file and the newspaper article I can't seem to stop reading about the case I can't stop thinking about.

Or the client I can't stop thinking about.

I push away from my desk and smooth out my skirt. "Awesome. I'm starved. Did you get that medical record release Jude Lawson signed over to Charlotte so she can make the request?"

Terri nods. "Yes, she's on it."

"Good." Making my way over to her, I glance across the hall to Schwartz's closed door. "He in with anyone?"

Terri shakes her head. "No. He's been holed up in there a while."

"He can probably use lunch, then." I hustle to his office, raise my hand, and rap my knuckles against the door, then open it without waiting for an answer. I stick in my head and dangle the bag. "Have you had lunch yet? I got your favorite from Ho Wop."

Schwartz sits up straighter in his leather chair, loosening the tie around his neck, and motions for me to enter. He glances at the desk drawer where I know he keeps a bottle of Johnny Walker Black as if he's considering that for lunch rather than the delicious Chinese food I brought him.

"What? No inappropriate comments or snide remarks? Are you sick?"

His usually bright eyes wear dark circles under them, and the way he was slumped in his chair when I first stuck my head in certainly didn't scream *I'm loving life and my job right now*.

I close the door behind me and make my way toward the sofa situated in the far-right corner of his office, depositing the bag full of takeout on the glass coffee table as I lower myself onto the couch. The firm, expensive leather dips with my weight, and I glance over at Schwartz, who still has barely acknowledged me.

Hell, I was just messing with him with my last comment, but maybe something really is wrong.

"You won't even answer me?"

He gives me an exasperated look.

"That doesn't bode well. Did someone die?"

"Sorry." He mutters the apology, swiping a hand over his face. "I've got a case that's haunting the fuck out of me."

Been there. Done that.

This area of law is always complicated. Everyone deserves the protections the Constitution grants, and it's up to us to ensure that the cops, the district attorneys, and everyone else on *that* side plays by the rules and gives our clients a fair shake, but that doesn't mean there aren't some cases—or clients—that get under your skin, from time to time.

Typically, it's the really violent fuckers who have no remorse, but sometimes, it's the really *human* ones who latch onto your soul. The people who are good deep down and simply made a mistake or got themselves into a situation they saw no way out of except to commit a crime.

It's not usual to see Schwartz struggle like this, though. Whatever the case is, it's bad. And despite my not-always-pleasant feelings toward the man, my heart aches for him and his discomfort.

He lumbers out of his chair and rounds the desk to join me on the sofa, walking with far less bravado than he normally does, almost looking defeated.

I study him for a moment as I remove the takeaway cartons from the bag and place them on the table in front of us. "Want to talk about it?"

"Not particularly." Schwartz hands me a pair of chopsticks from the bag, then browses the containers, ultimately reaching for the dumplings. "I've got Parrish's guy coming in soon to discuss his case."

That definitely isn't what his current mood is about, but I'll let the change in topic slide to avoid digging him deeper into whatever is bothering him. "How's that going?"

With both of our calendars stacked with cases, we haven't had a chance to see each other since Monday at the bar, and aside from a few texts with brief updates for him to pass along to Parrish about Enzo and Jude, we haven't even spoken.

Schwartz seems to consider the question like it doesn't have a simple answer like it should. In this office, "like shit" or "good" are the typical responses thrown around to that inquiry.

Ultimately, he shrugs. "They released him, for now. They're waiting on forensics. They got some DNA from the victim's nails and fingerprints from the hotel room, but the lab is so backed up, who knows how long it will be before they get any results."

"What about the hotel's security footage?" I pop a piece of General Tso's into my mouth.

"From what I could gather from my conversation with the ADA, they have him entering the hotel; that's it. The cameras on the floor of the victim's room weren't working."

"And yet, they still picked him up?"

Schwartz offers me an annoyed look. "They acted on an anonymous tip."

Of course they did...

There's a reason the Supreme Court of the United States has said that information provided anonymously must first be verified independently before it can be used as probable cause to arrest someone—because it's inherently unreliable.

I finish chewing the bite in my mouth and swallow. "Sounds like what they have so far is a total bullshit case."

"No argument there, and the ADA knows it, too."

The same thing that's been rattling around in my head since I learned the identity of the victims in our respective cases races to the forefront of my brain again.

"Though you have to admit, it's a little suspicious that your guy is a suspect in a case against my victim's business partner. I don't think it's a coincidence. Do you?"

Coincidences don't exist where Parrish and the Knights are involved. Two men attacked on the same night by assailants both tied to the Knights, and the victims are business partners...there's absolutely no way this wasn't part of some larger plan with a goal we aren't privy to or just can't see.

Something flashes across Schwartz's face for a second that makes it seem like maybe I'm the only one in the dark before he dips his head and takes a bite of a dumpling, shaking his head.

"I don't know what to make of it." He lowers the carton back to the table and turns to face me. "What's going on with the other two cases? I saw Brent Matthews' mug on the news this morning, something about him going in for surgery."

I dig inside the container with my chopsticks and pull out another piece of chicken. "Enzo swore to me that Matthews' ex-wife would corroborate his story about only acting in her defense after Matthews got rough with her. That's good for Enzo since it's an uphill battle when the victim is a damn congressional candidate.

"I'm hoping the negative light the statement from the ex will cast on Matthews will be enough for the case to go away so they can keep him squeaky clean for the election. Enzo seems like a clean-cut guy with no record, which is crazy considering who his father is.

"The only potential hiccup is that I did get the impression there is something going on between him and the ex-wife, or at the very least, there *was*. If it's true and it comes out, that would obviously raise a question about the veracity of any statement she makes to support his defense."

I toss the bite of chicken into my mouth and chew, thinking about all the potential ways Enzo's case could come back to bite me in the ass, the least of which is him actually going to prison and Wolf and the Knights showing up at my place to make me pay for my failure as counsel.

Schwartz leans back against the arm of the couch, considering what I just told him, apparently not as concerned for my life as I am. "And the other guy?"

Shit.

I pause the chopsticks at my mouth, then slowly lower them back into the container, releasing a heavy sigh. "The other guy is a pain in my ass."

One of Schwartz's dark eyebrows quirks. "Aren't they all?"

Chuckling humorlessly, I shake my head. "Oh, they definitely all are, but this one is a whole other level of complicated."

"How so?"

I lean back on the couch and release another exasperated sigh, thinking about Jude Lawson. "Well, for starters, he doesn't talk."

Schwartz chuckles this time. "Isn't that a dream client?"

A smirk pulls at my lips. "Ha ha. Yes, clearly, not speaking with the cops is a good thing, but the man literally doesn't talk to *anyone*. He had some major brain trauma when he was special ops, and it's apparently caused not only debilitating migraines but also a stutter so bad that rather than talk, he writes everything in a notebook."

"Seriously?"

I nod slowly. "I got him to talk to me briefly when I dropped him at his place, but he wasn't exactly chatty or forthcoming with anything. It's like pulling teeth, and I don't anticipate him cooperating or offering me anything that's going to really help me present a defense."

"Is there one?"

"I hope so." Leaning forward, I shrug. "Right now, all they have is two dead bodies and a homeless witness who heard shots from the roof of a building they caught my client coming out of."

"That isn't much."

"No." I shake my head. "It isn't, but ballistics on the bullets will narrow down the weapon type, and if it's something that comes from a sniper rifle, it's going to look very bad for the trained sniper. You know as well as I do that circumstantial evidence can still get someone convicted."

"Sounds like you've got a lot to keep you busy."

Understatement of the fucking year.

"Yeah, thanks for that." I elbow him playfully.

He just laughs and shakes his head.

It's nothing I can't handle, and he knows it. I thrive on the rush I get from deadlines and court and having people's lives in my hands. Some people crack under the pressure, but for me, it's my own brand of drug, one I can literally feel surging through my veins when I'm in "lawyer mode" and in my element.

But Jude Lawson is another thing altogether.

In all my years as an intern and then an attorney, I can't remember ever feeling this pull to a client, this *personal* desire to ensure he's protected.

Yeah, right, Finley. Tell yourself that's why you care so much.

The intercom sounds, and Charlotte's voice fills the air. "Your client is here."

That's my cue to leave.

Schwartz rises from the sofa and makes his way to his desk. "Send him in." He glances back to watch me pack up the barely-eaten Chinese.

"I'll get out of your hair."

"Thanks for lunch."

I wink at him. "No, thank you. I paid for it with the company card."

With that, I grab the bag and start for the door, but Charlotte opens it and ushers in Schwartz's client, allowing me to slip out and avoid being pulled into a meeting I want no part of.

There is enough going on with Enzo and Mouth, not

to mention the rest of my calendar. I don't need to be dragged into another Parrish case, one that's likely connected to Enzo's in some way I'm just not seeing yet.

At least one client doesn't appear to be tangled up in whatever it is.

Mouth may be *somehow* connected to Parrish—enough that the former president of the Satan's Knights sent me over there to help him—but there is no way there's a connection between the two men reportedly tied to the Russian mob who Mouth allegedly took out the other night and Brent Matthews or his partner, Guthrie.

That would just be *far* too "convenient"...and make my job a *lot* harder.

MOUTH

MY KNEE BOUNCES wildly on the rusted grate of the fire escape, and I take a deep inhale off my cigarette and hold the smoke in my lungs, allowing the nicotine to seep into my blood and spread through my body.

It's a nasty habit I've tried to kick at least a dozen times over the years, especially after my discharge, but unlike Chaos, who has his ex-wife-turned-current-wife to keep him on the straight and narrow, being here alone, cooped up in this apartment with nothing to do but surf the internet or binge watch shows I have little interest in, smoking again kind of became a given.

Over the years, my body just got too used to it as a way to relieve tension and relax. We all smoked like chimneys on deployments. It's an easy habit to fall back on at times like this. And being stuck here, the cravings were too much to ignore.

Thank fuck for Reaper.

It's almost like he knew exactly what I would need.

The man certainly knows how to take care of his people. Just like he always led us and watched over us when we were on Delta, he's still ensuring we have anything and everything we need now.

He rented the furnished apartment, ordered and shipped a computer, and ensured the Knights had stocked the place with necessities—including food and smokes—before I had even been released from jail.

All the things I would need to feel at home as much as possible while this fucking case plays out.

I should be able to relax, enjoy the time *off* with nothing to do, but this uneasiness isn't just about being caged up in here, like some dangerous animal threatening to bite. It's the entire situation—the whole reason I'm here—that has my mind running a mile a minute.

The fucking Russians...

I may have cut the head off the snake by taking out the newest Yankovich to grace New York with his smarmy presence, but there were other men at that warehouse. People I never got a shot at or *couldn't* take out before I hit the head man because it would alert him to the threat and might have made it possible for him to avoid my kind of retribution.

At least *some* of Maksim Yankovich's minions are still out there. Even if they're just hatchet men for the bratva, not the decision-makers pulling the strings, they can still be dangerous. They may figure out a way to revive the trafficking ring under new leadership or even resort to snatching women locally to satisfy the needs of their particular customers—the sick fucks who believe women are objects to be owned and traded and used like cattle.

Had things gone differently that night, had my body not betrayed me, I would have tracked them down elsewhere and taken them out by now. I'd be back in Baltimore helping Reaper and Chaos take out the remaining two men responsible for the assault on our client, Joanie.

Instead, I'm stuck here with this court-ordered hunk of jewelry strapped to my goddamn leg. I take another drag off my cigarette and let my eyes drift down to the green light, but it soon morphs into another shade surrounded by long, dark lashes and set on a beautiful face with flawless alabaster skin and lips I keep picturing wrapped around my cock.

Fuck.

Finley Banks.

That woman is pure fire.

The kind of roaring flame that lures you in close only to burn you.

It's a great quality to have in an attorney, but it wasn't her legal skills that kept me awake last night.

I can't stop thinking about how the remnants of my migraine evaporated being in that car with her; just simply sharing that space somehow eased the pain that had been plaguing me for days.

Nothing like that has ever happened before. Nothing but a lot of medication and time has ever offered me that kind of relief. Yet, half an hour in that enclosed space, breathing in her scent, allowing it to wash over me like a soothing balm, was all it took.

And by the time we pulled up outside this place, I practically leaped from the car to get away from her because of it.

If she hadn't called me back to sign that damn paper she said she needed to get my records, I wouldn't have even looked at her again before going into the building.

But I did go back, and she stood just outside her car, her brunette locks flowing in the breeze, looking every bit the beautiful girl next door every guy always has a crush on and not an attorney fighting for my life.

Fuck.

She's your lawyer, Mouth.

A fact I keep trying to remind myself of every time the parts of my brain that still work start to flash fantasies of her in very non-lawyerly positions in my head.

I take a final drag from my cigarette and stomp it out under my boot, then rise from my seat on the fire escape to climb back through the window and into the apartment—intent on finding *something* to do to occupy the brain I haven't been able to control for years.

My phone vibrates with an incoming message, and I pull it out and glance at the screen.

Reaper: Getting anxious yet?

I snort and shake my head as I type a reply. **What do you think?**

I think you're feeling like a caged animal.

Then you'd be right. There are still more vodka drinkers out there, and I left something someone needs to go recover.

That rifle must still be safely tucked behind the basement wall; otherwise, Finley would be alerting me to a major change in the status of the evidence in my case. But I won't risk leaving it there any longer than it needs to be, and with this damn monitor on my leg, I can't go back to dispose of it personally.

I knew you'd be concerned about both those things. I have Preacher looking into the first issue. He's checking for other names and locations. And I asked Parrish to send one of his guys to take care of the other problem.

Knowing the rifle will disappear relieves a little of the tension from my shoulders, but I still roll them, trying to dispel more of it before it brings on another migraine.

Is Chaos back from his second honeymoon yet?

A couple more days. They decided to stay a little longer.

Lucky bastard...

I'm happy for the fucker that he finally got back together with Avery after everything they've been through and found a slice of the happiness we all look for, but this second honeymoon is really bad fucking timing. Not only could Reaper use his help in finishing our job back in Baltimore, but having them here to assist with wrapping up the Russian problem would put a nice cap on something that should have ended when we were here a year ago.

If you're looking for something to occupy yourself with, I have another potential job from Parrish.

Fucking hell. What is it with this guy? The Knights can't handle their own shit anymore?

Apparently, some politician up there named Brent Matthews stole some money from one of their charities.

A man with a death wish.

No doubt. Only the guy they hired to do it fucked it up and got the dude's partner instead...and didn't finish the job.

That's what happens when you farm out your dirty work to cheap labor or unproven operators. You end up with some asshole who has no clue what he's doing and causes the kind of mistakes that can end up blowing back on a lot of people. The Knights are probably worried about this getting back to them.

What does Parrish want?

The partner, Guthrie, is in a coma, and they're looking for anything they can use to keep him quiet in case he wakes up.

That really isn't my department, and besides, I'm stuck here as long as I have this new anklet.

While Preacher does the deep dive on our Russian friends and this Guthrie guy for Parrish, he's also looking for a way to get you free of your new jewelry.

Is that possible?

We'll know soon enough. I'll keep you updated. Sit tight.

Like I have a fucking choice.

I shove my phone back into my pocket and work my way into the kitchen to pull a beer from the fridge. My bond conditions might say no consumption of alcohol, but if I'm going to be stuck here, I'm at least going to have a few beers.

Or more than a few.

Maybe if I drink enough of them, I'll stop remembering the way Finley looked at me before I climbed out of her car. And the way her hand felt on mine in that damn courtroom.

I pop off the cap and take three long, cool gulps of the hoppy liquid as I lean against the counter. My gaze drifts over the open floorplan of the loft apartment.

There are worse places to be stuck. Still, my skin itches and feels too tight, like it's suffocating me while I stand here. Like everything is closing in around me and will crush me under its weight.

I grab a second beer, pop the cap, and carry them back out through the window and onto the fire escape, the one place I can actually breathe the "fresh" New York air and, for just a second, close my eyes and pretend I'm somewhere else.

Out here, I have a good line of sight and the freedom to run if and when I need to. It's something that was ingrained in me at some point in my life I can't remember, a time I've only been told about by the few friends who still remained after the man they knew didn't come back.

With my eyes closed, the light breeze blowing against my face, flashes of memories come again.

Trees...

So many trees...

Woods...

A rifle in my hand...

My small hand...

This memory is older.

Childhood.

Maybe hunting with Dad and Grandpa.

A dull ache starts to form at the base of my skull, just like it typically does when I try to dig too much, try to drag up one of the old, fractured memories, and I reach back and massage it slowly, trying not to think about what I know would stop another migraine from coming.

The best thing I can do for myself and for Finley Banks is stay away from her as much as possible while this case is pending.

My phone vibrates again, but instead of Reaper's name, an unknown number flashes on the screen.

Only a handful of people on this planet have this number, and all of them would know not to call me and just to text. Unease slithers up my spine, and I slide my finger across the screen to answer the call, bringing the phone to my ear.

"Jude? Sorry, Mouth? It's Finley. Finley Banks, your attorney?"

Her unsteady voice rolls over me like a fog, enveloping me and clouding my brain instantly with that scent I can't forget and the tingle of her touch.

"You don't have to say anything. I just wanted to let you know that I should have the discovery in about a week—the police reports and photos of any other physical evidence they think they have. When I receive it, I'll want you to come into my office to review it with me. I have my paralegal trying to get those records you signed the release for."

She pauses for a moment, almost like she's expecting me to say something even though she explicitly told me it was fine not to.

"Um, in the meantime, if you need anything, just call or...I'm sorry, just text this number. It's my cell phone." Silence lingers on the line before she takes a sharp inhale. "Please call at any time, Mr. Lawson. Really. I'm worried about you."

The call ends, and I pull my phone away from my ear and stare at it, trying to process what just happened and what she just said. It takes a moment for her final words to click.

She's worried about me?

What the fuck does that mean?

My hand shakes, bringing the beer bottle to my lips, and I down the rest of the first one and set it down to immediately grab the second and drink half of it, too.

Finley Banks seems determined to get under my skin with her passion and compassion. I just have to make sure she doesn't succeed.

5

MOUTH

t's like these assholes want to die.

The heat of my anger blurs my vision and makes my hand tighten around the empty beer bottle as I take in the information on my computer screen that Preacher just sent over

I shove up from my seat on the couch and chuck it across the loft. It smashes against the exposed brick wall, glass shards exploding out across the worn wood floor with a satisfying sound.

Fucking hell.

I flex my fists at my sides, wanting so badly to escape this cage and go after these fuckers to see they get what they deserve.

And what they deserve is a fucking hole blown through them.

These guys are definitively tied to the Yankovich

crew, and they're definitely dangerous.

Three came over from Russia with the cousin. Three more who were low-ranking associates here, under the previous Yankovich, and who managed to escape the retribution we enacted against them last year. Six too many terrible people still alive and out on the streets, still potential threats to the innocent people of New York and beyond. Because these fuckers don't keep things within the city limits.

They're bringing in girls from all around the world. Their dirty hands touch people everywhere, and no matter what we do, it seems like it may be never-ending.

We thought we had taken care of it before, believed we had eliminated their entire operation here in a way that not only ensured it would never be resurrected but that also sent a message to anyone stupid enough to try.

Yet now, these fuckers are rearing their ugly, sinister heads again. All while Chaos is out on his goddamn second honeymoon and Reaper needs to stay in Baltimore to continue to keep an eye on Joanie and Viktoria, who is still not back to one hundred percent after what happened when Avery ran back into Chaos' life so unexpectedly.

That means these fuckers are *my* responsibility, and there's not a damn thing I can currently do about it.

I glance down at the green light flashing on my ankle. It continues to taunt me, a constant reminder of how badly I fucked up that night. A reminder of how badly my body betrayed me and left me vulnerable to mistakes.

It keeps me tied here, stuck with my regret, my broken memories, and the constant flow of information from Preacher that only confirms my worst fears—these guys are unlikely to disappear just because I took out Maksim Yankovich.

Since Preacher hasn't had any luck so far in hacking the system that controls the GPS monitor and anti-tampering portion of this plastic manacle, it means all I can do is pace and take out my frustrations on unsuspecting beer bottles and myself.

My phone buzzes with a text from Preacher.

Check out what I just emailed you.

A part of me dreads what it might be, what other horrific things he's dredged up, but I need all the information if I'm ever going to be able to move against them.

Even if it makes my head throb and my entire body so rigid that it's about to snap in half.

I lower myself back to the couch and click on the attachment on Preacher's email.

Bank records pop up—huge cash transactions of fifty up to three hundred thousand dollars at a time. Many of them happening on the same dates over a number of years.

What am I looking at?

I tracked down some bank accounts on some of the fuckers you guys took out last year while I was trying to look for anybody alive who is still connected to them. This one stood out. It's an offshore account in the Bahamas. Look at the dates on page two.

I scroll down past a blur of numbers, and my blood runs cold.

Holy shit.

I grab my phone and fire off a text.

That was the date of the last auction. The one that happened before we came to New York.

Exactly. This is where all the money from the auctions was going.

Holy shit. Can you trace the deposits to who made the purchases?

Purchases...

What we're talking about are women. Some mere girls. Innocents stolen from their lives and families and sold into sexual slavery to wealthy, evil, and entitled men.

Working on it. And I have a friend helping me with your little jewelry situation.

I snort and shake my head, rolling out my ankle under the coffee table.

Good. It isn't really my style.

Didn't think so, buddy. I'll have more for you soon.

It better be a message saying he figured out how to get this damn monitor off because I don't know how much longer I can stay in here. I set down my phone and click back over to the original information Preacher sent me on the remaining Russians.

Six is doable, even without Reaper and Chaos or anyone else here—as long as I can get out of this place without the court knowing I'm violating my bond.

My gaze drifts over to the crate in the corner of the

room that was delivered only a few hours ago. With the necessities the guys just sent me, I'll have everything I need to continue my original mission here. The one that was so rudely interrupted by that fucking migraine that ruined everything.

I push up from the couch and stretch my back and neck, cracking and popping audibly the same way they have every single day since the explosion that knocked me off the roof of the building and destroyed my life as I knew it. And now, the new life I've created with Reaper and Chaos, protecting innocent people, helping them find peace through justice they can't get any other way, could all be over.

Reaper put so much faith in me to do this job, and I fucked it up.

If I get put away for this...

I shake my head, trying to clear that thought from my mind, but the one that immediately replaces it isn't much better—the stunning attorney fighting to make sure that doesn't happen.

The way her light, reassuring touch simultaneously sends shivers and heat racing through my body. The way my cock stirred to life for the first time in years.

Christ, like it's doing right now just thinking about it.

I reach down and adjust my cock away from behind my zipper as I make my way toward the window to stare out at the street below. Staten Island is quiet this time of night, especially in this area.

Reaper definitely picked a good place to have me stay until this is resolved. I'd much rather be at the safe house we usually use when we're in New York, but we need to keep that place hidden and available whenever we need it—not listed on record with the damn court.

This is only temporary.

Hopefully.

If the fiery brunette with the kind smile and soft touch has anything to say about it, I'll be back in Baltimore and returning to my life there soon.

I reach up and grab the lintel, leaning forward to watch the occasional car or pedestrian move along down the street or sidewalk. People just living their lives. People with families and memories.

Things I'll never have. Things I never *can* have. Things everyone else takes for granted.

Like Abigail and Michaela.

Even my own sisters are strangers to me, which is why I pushed them away when I woke up and didn't recognize them. No number of stories from growing up together would jog my fractured memory. No amount of "unconditional love" would return to me what was stolen by that RPG. So, I fought them and their efforts. I kept them at arm's length, and that length grew and grew until they were no longer coming to see me. Until I made it clear I didn't want them to. Until the only people left in my life were the ones I did have fleeting memories of—Reaper and Chaos. The people who helped explain to me who I was, even if I never truly remember it. What they said, what they told me about *that* life was the only thing that ever seemed right, that ever seemed real.

I can't lose it to get locked away in a real cage some-where. I won't let that happen.

And I won't let these feelings raging inside me about my damn attorney get in the way of letting her do her job.

A familiar car pulls up to the curb in front of the building, and my chest tightens immediately, my heart beating rapidly against my ribcage.

What the hell is she doing here?

FINLEY

I STARE up at the building and the window of the apartment where Mouth is staying. I don't want to call it his because it really isn't.

It's just temporary.

Like this feeling I get around him that is sure to dissipate.

Just a place Reaper rented for him to ensure the court was going to let him out on bond, but even just looking at the darkened window, I can almost feel his presence sizzling across my skin. That blue assessing gaze that seems to see everything even though he says nothing.

And I can't blame him for wanting to remain silent. With everything he has been through, all that he has suffered, why would he want to engage in a conversation with someone when he doesn't have to?

But it makes it impossible to gauge his state of mind

or know how he's doing—alone, injured, facing something that could send him away for the rest of his life.

I glance at the paper bag on the passenger seat.

This is stupid, Finley. What the fuck are you doing?

It's the same question I've been asking myself for the last half an hour ever since I walked out of Malicious Meatballs with two subs, two fries, and a plan to come to see my most intriguing and frustrating client.

Turn around.

Go home.

Forget about Jude Lawson until you have to talk to him about the case.

Despite knowing how wrong it is, I still turn off the ignition. I still grab the bag and step from the car. What I should do is drive over to Charlotte's and make sure she's okay after the Braxton Hicks excitement earlier today.

I almost wish I had been there just to see Schwartz freaking out and having to drive our pregnant paralegal to the hospital when she thought she was in labor. She would likely appreciate what I have in this bag since it's been one of her pregnancy cravings, but something tells me the man in that apartment needs it more.

Or maybe I do and I'm just making excuses for my reckless actions.

I scan the street with some ridiculous fear there might be someone out here who would know I have no business being at my client's residence at eight o'clock on a Friday fucking night.

Of course, no one's watching me.

The only other person on the street, a single pedestrian with a dog, walks in the opposite direction, likely heading home to settle in for the evening. Still, I feel eyes on me from somewhere. I peer back up at the window.

No, it can't be.

There wouldn't be any reason for him to be watching me. It's just my own self-consciousness making me crazy.

I shake off the feeling, lock the car, and make my way into the lobby. Staring at the buzzer for his apartment number, I shift nervously from foot to foot. This is my last chance to turn around. To walk back to my car, drive to Charlotte's to share this or home, and gorge on this entire bag of food. I'd surely regret it tomorrow, but maybe not as much as reaching up and pressing the buzzer button.

Instead of a greeting, just the soft crackle that tells you someone picked up comes through the line.

"Jude…Mouth. Sorry, it's me." *Shit.* "It's Finley. I brought you something. I know it's a Friday night, but—"

The buzzer sounds on the door to my left, and I quickly grab the handle and pull it open to gain access to the main lobby. Each step I take should be one in the opposite direction, but the elevator dings, and the doors slide open, almost as if in welcome.

A woman carrying a small white dog steps out and offers me a smile. "Good evening."

"Hi. Have a nice night." I slip into the elevator and punch the button for the fourth floor, then lean back against the metal interior and squeeze my eyes shut. The crinkle of my hand tightening around the paper bag fills the tight space, adding to the rushing of my blood in my ears.

What the hell are you doing, Finley?

My knee bounces.

This is a professional visit.

I'm checking on a client who has no other connections here.

No one to rely on and who has a serious medical condition.

That's it.

I nod sharply to no one, almost as if it will convince me that's true.

The elevator pings, and the doors slide open. I suck in a deep breath and push off the wall, stepping out into the hallway and up to his apartment.

Shit. Shit. Shit.

I raise my hand and lightly knock. The door opens immediately, and Mouth stands there as if he has been waiting for me the whole time. His icy-blue gaze meets mine, and he raises an eyebrow.

His way of questioning my sudden appearance at his place without having to actually voice it.

Hell. I wish I had an answer.

I offer an awkward smile and hold up the bag. "Hi. I worried you might not know the good local places to eat." When he doesn't offer a response, I shrug. "I thought I'd introduce you to one of my favorite spots."

His gaze drops to the bag in my hand and the words "Malicious Meatballs" written on the front of the brown paper.

"Meatball subs and fries..."

Silence spreads between us, and he slowly lifts his head until he's piercing me with those Caribbean blues again. He takes a half step back and opens the door, making room for me to enter.

Shit. Shit. Shit.

I force each step forward, and the door clicks closed behind me, making me jump and look over my shoulder at him as he approaches to my left. He walks past me without a word and over to the kitchen counter with four high stools. I follow him cautiously, scanning the loft space.

Nice but not extravagant.

He'll be comfortable here until his case gets resolved.

And hopefully, he's not heading off to a new place with bars after this.

If I do my job well and if things pan out the way I hope they will, he won't be.

I set the bag on the counter and slide on to one of the stools, unsure what I'm supposed to be doing as he moves to the refrigerator and tugs it open. The hard muscles of his back punch and flex under the tight T-shirt stretched over wide shoulder blades, and my tongue darts out across my lips, imagining what he must look like under all of that.

He turns back toward me, holding two beers, his biceps bulging, and knocks the fridge shut with his foot. Holding up one of the bottles, he raises a brow.

Alcohol sounds good right now. Though, lowering my inhibitions around this man is probably the last thing I should be doing. Still, I nod because I can't seem to think rationally when I'm around my client.

Client. Client. Client.

If I think the word enough, it might remind me why I'm here and what he is.

He pops the caps off with a bottle opener and tosses it back into the drawer, then moves around the counter to slide on to the stool next to me. Almost instantly, my body becomes aware of how close he is, the heat radiating off him mixing with a heavy, masculine scent—like leather and gunpowder.

I don't realize I'm staring until his eyes connect with mine, and he quirks a brow again.

"Oh." I turn back to the bag in front of me and pull it open, the heat of a flush over my cheeks assuring me they're already bright red. "So, like I said"—I point toward the name on the bag—"Malicious Meatballs has the best meatballs on Staten Island. To be honest, I probably shouldn't eat them as much as I do. I don't need that many calories in my life. But they're addictive."

And I'm rambling.

He narrows his eyes on me, his reproach about the calorie comment evident without him saying a word.

Damn this man.

I swallow thickly, pull out the sandwiches and fries, and arrange them in front of us. He unwraps his while I glug three long drinks from my beer. The smell of the delicious meatballs, sauce, and freshly baked bread hits me, and my mouth begins to water more than I already did at the scent emanating from the man next to me.

Mouth digs in and takes a bite, and a little apprecia-tive groan comes from deep in his throat.

Sweet Mother of God. That sound...

My pussy clenches, imagining him making that sound for other reasons, and I shift on the stool to relieve the pressure building there.

I take a way-too-big bite of my sandwich to fill my mouth and prevent myself from saying something stupid. Chewing, I chance a glance at him, and it's my turn to raise an eyebrow at his assessing gaze locked on me. "Good?"

He mouths "*very*" to me, and I can't fight the grin, knowing he's enjoying it.

This is the most relaxed I've seen the man, and he offers a half-smile that tilts his perfect lips.

Mouth.

That name can mean so many things. And now, I can't stop thinking about what they could be—one in particular.

He takes another bite and chews slowly, his strong jaw working under several days of stubble. I shove a French fry into my mouth, and his tongue snakes out across his lips to catch the sauce there.

I practically choke and start coughing violently, pounding on my chest and grabbing my beer to wash down my embarrassment.

Good God, I'm in trouble.

6

FINLEY

"**A**re you freaking insane?" Laura's eyes practically bug out of her head, and she almost spills her coffee. "You brought a client food and went into his apartment alone? Were you high or something?"

I groan and shake my head, her reproach almost as bad as what I've been doing to myself since I left his place last night. "No. I definitely feel like I was possessed by something, though."

Some sort of supernatural power that draws me to a dangerous man who very likely just murdered two people and has killed countless more in his life.

"You must have been because you're not dumb, Finley. You're probably the smartest person I know. But that is just fucking *stupid*. That's how you cross a line.

That's how you get your license suspended or worse—end up disbarred or dead."

I slam my palm against the table. "You think I don't fucking know that?"

She recoils slightly, her jaw dropping incredulously, while a couple at the table next to us in the small coffee shop gives me a dirty look.

"I'm sorry." I shake my head and groan, reaching across the table to squeeze her hand. "I didn't mean to snap at you. This guy...just...I don't know. He just *unnerves* me."

Her bourbon eyes widen. "That's saying a lot considering the type of people you work with on a daily basis."

I nod slowly, take a sip of my double latte, and casually pick at the half-eaten doughnut on my plate. The one I *should* be enjoying considering it's our Saturday tradition once we finish pilates class, but I can't even bring myself to eat it when all I can think about is what happened last night.

"Well"—she raises a blond eyebrow at me—"what happened?"

Nothing and everything.

Somehow, it was both, and I don't even know how to explain it to her.

I glance around us to make sure no one's eavesdropping and lean forward slightly closer so I don't have to talk so loudly. "I showed up with some Malicious Meatball subs."

Her eyes roll back in her head, and she licks her lips. "God, they're good."

"I know, which is why I brought it to him. He doesn't have anyone here, Laura. He has no friends, no family. He can't leave the apartment because he's on electronic monitoring from the court."

"That's why they invented grocery and food delivery, Finley. It's called Uber Eats."

I twist my lips at her jibe. "I know. But I've been worrying about him being alone in there with his medical issues and this case hanging over his head."

"What type of a case is it?"

Crap.

I brace myself for her reaction. With as busy as she's been at the hospital all week, I'm sure she didn't see anything on the news about it even though the death of the current head of the Russian bratva definitely drew a lot of attention and had Mouth's name splashed all over the newspaper due to his arrest. I close my eyes and force the words out. "Double homicide."

"Are you fucking *nuts*, woman?"

The same couple next to us glares again.

Laura turns to them. "Oh, you two—stop eavesdropping." She returns her attention to me. "You went into the apartment of a man accused of double homicide—by yourself—to bring him a fucking sandwich because you were *worried*. Girl, you need to get checked out by a mental health professional—stat."

"I know how it looks, how it sounds, but I swear he's—"

"He's what?" Her eyebrows rise. "A killer?"

"Not sure yet." I drum my fingers on the table and take another sip of my drink. "At this point, it's *allegedly*."

She snorts. "Your favorite word."

"That's because everyone is entitled to the benefit of the doubt. Innocent until proven guilty."

"Sure, of course, but if they charged him with *homicide*, they must have some evidence suggesting he did it."

"He was found at the location they *think* the shooter set up at, and he was military special ops. One of those people you're not supposed to know about unless you have some sort of top-secret security clearance."

"Are you fucking kidding me?"

I shake my head. "And he's charged with killing two Russian mobsters."

"Holy shit."

When you hear it out loud, it *does* sound bad. Really bad. About as bad as any case I've worked on. But Mouth isn't like any client I've ever had. His silence forces me to actually *see* him, and what I see isn't what others think he is.

"I don't know what it is about this guy, Laura. He just doesn't seem like someone who would commit cold-blooded murder."

She shifts forward slightly and glances at the eaves-dropping couple. "Well, they have enough to charge him..."

"Yeah, but not enough to convict—at least based on what I've seen so far. I'll get the discovery next week sometime and be able to review all the police reports. All

I have right now is the criminal complaint which is really a bare-bones summary of their case."

"So, the guy *maybe* killed two Russian mobsters, could kill *you* and anyone else with a fucking toothpick, and you felt inclined to bring him a meatball sub? Sure, that seems totally sane to me."

She takes a sip of her tea and gives me a look I know all too well.

"I could do without the sarcasm, Laura."

I'm already dealing with two major cases that are going to be a pain in my ass on top of the caseload I was already weighed down with before that two a.m. call from Schwartz that sent me down this fucked-up avenue in the first place.

How do I describe this to her without sounding more like a lunatic than I already do?

"He's...he's complicated." I glance up and meet her concerned gaze. "He doesn't talk."

Her brow furrows. "What do you mean *he doesn't talk*?"

"He has a traumatic brain injury from when he served. That's why he was discharged, and it causes him to stutter badly, badly enough that he doesn't want to talk."

"Hell"—her shoulders sag, and she frowns—"that's kind of sad."

"It is." I shake my head and drop my focus to my donut again. "But it's not that I feel bad for him. Because I don't. This isn't a sympathy thing. I'm just drawn to him in some way that makes me want to help him and ensure he's okay."

"You mean as an attorney to her client?"

I finally let my gaze meet hers. "I don't know. That's the problem."

"Shit." She releases a mirthless laugh. "You have yourself in some deep fucking water. Does Schwartz know anything about this?"

I shake my head. "God, no. If he knew, he'd probably pull me off the fucking case. But he's tied up with an attempted homicide of his own and several other big cases. It's not like he could step in, anyway."

"So, what are you going to do?"

I shrug and take a sip of my now-cold drink. "I guess just try to keep things professional."

She scowls at me. "*Try* to keep things professional. That does not instill a lot of confidence."

Then this won't, either.

But now that I've opened the floodgates of discussing Jude Lawson, I can't seem to stop. Laura is the only person I ever discuss my personal life with, and she's the only one I can count on to remain absolutely brutally honest with me when I come to her for advice.

"The thing is...I don't totally trust him."

"Nor should you, Fin. He is likely a murderer."

I flick my gaze to hers. "But what if the people he killed deserved it?"

Her eyes widen. "Did I really just hear those words come out of your mouth?"

"I know, I know how crazy it sounds."

"I don't think you do, Finley. This guy is potentially a double murderer who certainly has the background and training to have done it. There's enough evidence to charge him, yet you're showing up to bring him dinner on a Friday night. You need to get a grip, or you're gonna end up drowning in that deep water."

What if I already am?

MOUTH

I NEVER TRULY APPRECIATED WHAT freedom meant until I lost it.

All the years I served, everything I saw, all the horrors and mistreatments, I thought it had given me a deep understanding of it—of its cost, of what it means to those who never had it, of how lucky I was to never have to worry about my own. But it only took two days of being restricted in the condo to drive me absolutely mad as if it had been two decades.

By the time Preacher texted me earlier tonight to tell me he had hacked the monitor and could set me free, I was practically crawling out of my own skin.

I roll out my ankle, relishing the feeling of having that stupid thing off. Now that it's safely back at the condo, green lights still active so they think I'm there, it allows me to get out *here* and do what I do best.

Work on taking out these nasty motherfuckers.

Our vodka-drinking friends don't suspect anything.

They sit in the restaurant across the street, laughing, joking, stuffing their guts with food and booze, not a care in the world. Completely unaware they're already in my crosshairs and will soon be dead.

Other patrons move in and out of the building, either oblivious to the fact that these horrible men sit right out in the open or ignoring it to ensure their own personal safety—likely the latter. In this neighborhood, there isn't anyone who doesn't know who these guys are and what they're capable of.

A couple holding hands exits and makes their way to their car in the parking lot next door, but they aren't the ones I'm waiting for.

Two of the men who escaped me the other night emerge a few moments later, chatting as they share a cigarette near the front door. Neither of them seems to have a care in the world, even though their boss was just taken out less than a week ago.

Probably because they know I was arrested. Had I remained in custody, had Finley not been able to get me on bond, they would have undoubtedly sent someone after me on the inside to try to take me out. One of their guys or a cop on their payroll. It wouldn't have worked, but these guys weren't smart enough to move fast, and they certainly aren't smart enough to be afraid now.

The taller of the two leans against the brick of the building and takes a long drag from his cigarette. He releases the smoke in a ring that floats over his head into the night sky.

After hours of being up here and doing recon on the

place, it's clear the restaurant is a front for the bratva and likely laundering money from the account we found. And while I would love to pull the trigger right now so there would be two fewer scumbags out on the street, that's not what tonight is about.

It's about watching, waiting, and planning to ensure what happened when I took out their boss doesn't happen again.

This will be an easy place to eliminate them. At least four of the men on that list have come and gone tonight. All I have to do is wait until they're all here at the same time to give myself the opportunity to hit as many as possible.

I climb to my feet and step away from the low wall around the roof that I used to conceal myself, scanning my phone for messages. Secretly hoping there will be one from a certain woman who left my head spinning last night with her impromptu visit and quick, awkward exit.

Preacher: Call me. You're not going to believe what I found.

Shit.

If Preacher wants me to call him, it's far too detailed or important for him to tell me in a text message.

Hopefully good news.

I slowly wander back toward where I parked the car I rented under one of my aliases. Nothing more than an average Brighton Beach resident out for a lovely stroll on a summer night. I dial as I walk, bringing the phone to my ear as I approach my ride.

Preacher answers on the first ring. "I found something you're absolutely going to love or hate, depending on how you look at it."

I snort and slide into the car, closing the door behind me.

"So, you know how Reaper called me to have me look into this Guthrie guy for Parrish? Well, those accounts I was tracking down that made the deposits at the same time as the auction...guess who one of them belongs to?"

I freeze with my hand at the ignition. "Holy s-s-shit."

"Yeah, my reaction, too. The guy was one of the original buyers in the auction the month before you guys came in and tore the place apart."

This fucker Parrish wants dirt on was buying women. And his business partner was apparently embezzling money from a charity. It can't be a coincidence. Perhaps it's the reason Matthews stole from the Knights in the first place. Undoubtedly, all sorts of sketchy things were going on with both of these guys in order to support what must be a very expensive and nasty habit.

"I already relayed this all to Reaper, and he says he's likely going to have you meet with Parrish in person to explain it because he's about to go dark for a while doing recon on something else you have going on in Baltimore."

Likely final planning for taking out those last two fuckers for Joanie as soon as Chaos gets back.

"I wanted to let you know right away because now that you're a somewhat free man, I thought it might not be a bad idea to have you look to see if you can find out what happened to the girl while you're there in town."

My heart climbs into my throat, considering the possibilities.

That was such a long time ago when it comes to this world. So much could have happened to her. Chances are, she isn't with Guthrie or even in the city anymore. She might not even be alive.

The men who frequent those types of auctions often trade women based on their changing whims and preferences, letting others use them for their own pleasure while destroying them bit by bit until they finally can't take it anymore and do what they must to escape permanently—one way or another.

"I'm seeing what I can find from my end, but I'm texting you all the addresses I have for Guthrie. With him in the hospital, I would imagine it should be pretty easy to get in and out of these places."

There goes my plan to head back to the condo.

But I couldn't go sit on that damn couch or try to sleep knowing what I do now—that there might be an innocent woman somewhere in the city who has been abused by Guthrie—and God only knows who else—for the better part of a year. Though, even if Preacher hadn't just shaken me with this news, it would be better that I don't go back to my place now that it smells like Finley.

That light, citrusy-mint fragrance has lingered since she left last night. After I had to watch her eat that goddamn sandwich.

Her lips closing around it...

Her tiny little noises of pleasure...

All while I pictured her doing the same with my cock.

Fuck.

Knock it off, Mouth.

She's your attorney...

Who brought you dinner on a Friday night...

I fire up the ignition and pull away from the curb, heading toward the first address on the list of Guthrie's properties from Preacher.

She's just worried about you.

She told you exactly that the other day.

Someone calling or texting to check in because they're worried is one thing...bringing them dinner and sitting and eating with them is another. And that's exactly what she did, just inhaled that whole foot-long like she was a deep-throating champ while interjecting one-sided small talk without expecting me to respond, seemingly unfazed by my silence.

It felt too natural, too real, too easy.

This woman literally holds my life in her hands, but I feel her touching other parts of me. Parts I thought died in that explosion. Parts I can't give her.

If this mission fails, a lot of very bad people are going to continue to do a lot of very bad things.

Finley is one distraction I can't afford.

7

MOUTH

The buzzer sounds, and I make my way over and thumb the button to unlock the lobby door without even checking who it is. Only a handful of people know I'm here, so it's either Parrish, one of his guys, or Finley again.

That last possibility suddenly tenses every muscle in my body. Maybe I should have looked so I could have at least prepared myself to see her, to have her in this space with me, steel myself against what I know being near her will do to me.

Too fucking late now.

A bang sounds on the door. "Knock, knock, moth-erfucker."

I release a tiny breath of relief at the sound of Parrish's voice through the wood. I'd rather deal with that asshole than Finley right now.

God, that's fucked up.

I flip the lock and open the door, stepping back to allow him to amble in.

He scans the apartment and nods approvingly. "Nice place. What are you going to do with it when you're done?"

I shrug and pull out the notebook from my back pocket that I already wrote in to prepare for this meeting. It would have been a lot easier for Reaper to just call Parrish with this information, but he needs to concentrate on our client back home. This is my mess, and after Parrish got me an attorney, the obligation to assist with this Guthrie issue weighs heavily on my shoulders, as much as I hate owing this man anything.

Plus, while I trust that everything I say to Preacher and the guys is secure, we don't know shit about Parrish's phone or who might be listening in or watching him. In-person assures there aren't any listening ears or prying eyes.

I flip open the first page and turn it to him.

He scans it and lifts a brow, pulling the toothpick from his mouth. "You have something on Guthrie?"

Nodding, I motion for him to follow me into the kitchen, where that same minty scent still lingers even two days later. That fucking woman is messing with my head, and I haven't even touched her yet.

No, not YET.

You're not GOING to touch her—ever.

A fact I have been reminding myself of continuously

since I watched her car drive away after our meal the other night.

I grab two beers, pop them open, and slide one across the counter to Parrish. He takes a sip as I flip to the next page in my book and turn it toward him.

Our guy dug up some financial information on the Russians we never had before. And guess who he found on the original buyers list from the auctions before we shut them down?

Parrish's jaw drops. "You're fucking kidding me."

I shake my head and motion for him to turn the page.

He wired $250,000 to the Yankovich bank account the same night we know an auction happened.

"Holy shit. Maybe that's why Matthews was embezzling the money from Frankie's House? Were they both involved?"

I shrug and pull the notebook away from him, flip to a blank page, and scribble in it.

I don't know anything about that. Just that Guthrie bought a girl. Our guy, Preacher, is trying to find her, and I have been scoping out a few of the remaining Russians and also swung by Guthrie's place to see if there was any sign of her there.

Taking a drink, I slide the note over to him and wait for him to read it. I could probably just tell him all this. It would make it a lot faster and a lot easier, but the thought of exposing my weakness to a guy like Parrish, who likely has none, makes my blood run cold.

Not that he doesn't likely know by now after Finley exposed me in court but knowing and actually experiencing and seeing it are two different things.

"How the fuck did you get out of here"—he scans the apartment and glances at my leg where the lights still flashes green—"with that still on?"

I grin at him and mouth the word "*magic.*"

He barks out a laugh, shakes his head, and takes a sip of his beer. "Man, you guys are something else. I respect the creativity."

I grab the notebook and scribble, twisting it back to him.

I'll take that as a compliment.

"You should."

As much as I enjoy having the company and the distraction from constantly fantasizing about my damn attorney, I'm ready to get things moving in the direction of some sort of resolution.

What's the plan?

Parrish's lip curls into a sneer, and he takes a drink of his beer, letting the bottle dangle from his fingertips. "I don't run the show over there anymore, unfortunately. Frankie's House is near and dear to the Knights, so the fact that this asshole was likely involved with Matthews stealing from us put a target on his back already. Now with this new information about the auctions..." He pauses for a second, drumming his fingers on the counter. "You know, Matthews was out in Brighton Beach the other night. Supposedly, he was visiting his girl-friend, but that could be a cover."

Not everyone in Brighton Beach is connected to Russian bratva.

"But it's definitely an interesting coincidence."

I nod and consider what I found last night while snooping around Guthrie's house. There was certainly a lot of indication that he and Matthews were tight, practically attached at the hip. I doubt one did anything without the other knowing about it. So even if they weren't both actively involved with each other's crimes, they certainly had knowledge and did nothing to stop them.

That puts targets on *both* their backs, as far as I'm concerned.

I write down as much and flip it over to Parrish.

He nods. "That's what I thought as well. Thanks again for doing this."

I turn to the last page I already wrote before he even came.

I'm working on cleaning out the rest of our Russian problem.

Parrish smiles and sticks that damn toothpick back into his mouth. "Good. Don't want these fuckers starting shit up here again. Twice was enough."

I snort and nod.

It sure was.

"As far as I know, Guthrie is still in a coma, and they're not sure if he is going to wake up. If he does, you may need to go in there and work your magic so it doesn't land back on us."

I make the slitting throat motion, but he shakes his head.

"No, just a threat to keep him quiet. The cops already have their eye on the guy who fucked up the whole thing. If Guthrie dies, it's a murder charge that could come back to the Knights. If he lives but doesn't reveal anything about who did it, the prick can walk and we'll be in the clear."

My hand tightens on the bottle. Going in to take out a scumbag like Guthrie is the kind of thing I live for. Not being able to end him will certainly put a damper on that, but at least I can fuck with the man and make him live the rest of his days in constant fear.

I flip to an open page and write, grinning at Parrish.

It would be my fucking pleasure. Just tell me when and where.

FINLEY

THE COUPLE on the TV embrace and kiss, the hero swinging the heroine around in her white wedding dress while the sun sets behind them and dramatic music designed to make you cry and question your own life plays in the background.

And it's working.

I don't usually fall into the "watches sappy romance movies" category, but flipping through channels aimlessly tonight, something about the story on the screen drew me in.

Maybe because it's about as far from how I've pictured my future for so long that it's completely foreign. Work is my life, and I never even considered what putting off relationships would mean for me ten or twenty years down the line.

I didn't think I cared, but the tears pooling in my eyes seem to suggest otherwise.

Don't be a fucking sap, Finley.

My phone vibrates with an incoming text, and I swipe at my eyes and hold my breath before I flip the screen to face me, a huge part of me hoping to see Mouth's number there.

Rick: Talked to Matthews' ex-wife. You got a minute to talk about it?

My stomach tightens.

That doesn't sound good.

Rick knows better than to call me on a Sunday unless it's urgent, and urgent usually means *bad* news—the kind that will keep me up all night and make my job a lot harder. As a former cop and private investigator for the firm, Rick has seen it all over the years and knows how to judge a witness, and he almost *never* calls me with information he can easily provide to me tomorrow in the office.

I turn off the TV and type a response to him.

Yeah, I'm around.

My phone rings almost immediately, and I slide my finger across it to answer the call. "Hey, what's going on?"

"I know how much you hate to work on the weekend if you can avoid it, but I talked to Danica Matthews, and I just got done typing up my report. I thought you might want to know the results quickly on this one, considering who your victim is."

I release a tiny breath of relief. "So, it isn't bad news, then?"

"No, quite the contrary. Danica Matthews is going to be a very good witness for you and make the State's case against Enzo a lot harder."

"Why?" I shift up into a sitting position. "What did she say?"

"Basically, the exact same thing Enzo did. She confirmed that she attended the fundraiser with her ex-husband and that she's continued to appear with him at these events—not because she still has feelings for him or anything like that, but because she didn't want to tank his campaign. Now, here's where I think she was holding a little something back."

"Okay."

I figured there had to be *something*. Nothing is ever clear-cut in these situations.

"She says they got into an argument at the event and that he tried to leave before they had finished their conversation."

"What were they arguing about?"

"She wouldn't say—said it was a personal, private matter."

I wince. "That doesn't sound good."

"Might not be, but she says she followed him because the conversation needed to happen that night. He pulled up outside the house out in Brighton Beach, and she confronted him again. That's when he attacked her."

"She used the word *attacked*?"

"Most certainly did."

"Excellent."

"He lunged at her and grabbed her by the throat."

"Damn, some potential congressman, huh?"

Rick snorts. "Exactly the thought I had. Anyway, she says, suddenly, somebody was pulling Matthews off her, and when she managed to break away from the scuffle for a moment, she realized it was Enzo."

"And how does she know Enzo?"

That's the ultimate question, one I never got a satisfactory answer to from my client at the jail.

"She claims they know each other because Matthews hired him to do some repair work on a boat they shared when they were still married."

"That's it? That's all she said?"

"That's all she said. But you know me too well and know I have some extra thoughts."

I chuckle at him, dropping my head back against the couch. "I know. Lay it on me, Detective."

He chuckles. "I *do* think she was holding something back, either about the reason for the argument or about Enzo."

"I agree with you." Thinking back to Enzo's reaction when I made the suggestion, there was definitely something off about his reaction. "There may be something going on between the two of them, if not currently, then in the past. Do you think she had an affair with him while she was married to Matthews?"

"Can't say and she didn't want to expand on her relationship with Enzo, just brushed it off as being acquaintances because he did the repair work on the boat."

"But she's willing to testify that a US congressional candidate attacked her and tried to strangle her?"

"Yep, everything else is all just a feeling and supposition on our part."

Exactly.

Which means the State won't be able to prove it, either. If there were something out there to find about Danica and Enzo, then Rick would find it. The man is relentless, like a bloodhound sniffing out the truth. He goes far beyond what the State does when looking into these witnesses and their backgrounds, so if he hasn't located anything damning, it might not exist. And if it does, it's so well-buried that it's unlikely to surface.

"Okay. Email me your report tonight so I can read over exactly what she said. Call her tomorrow and have her come in and sign an affidavit to that effect. Can you type it up for her, or should I have Charlotte do it based on your report?"

"I can do it tonight."

"Right, get it to Charlotte. Tell Danica to come into the office and sign it whenever it's convenient for her."

"Will do, Fin, but I didn't even get to tell you the best part."

That perks me up. "What's that?"

"We're not just going to have this statement."

"What do you mean? Was there another witness?"

"Not that I know of, but Danica says the night it happened, she had to leave the scene. I don't know what she meant by 'had to leave.' But my guess is Enzo told her to before the cops arrived. When she realized they had arrested Enzo even though he was only protecting her, she apparently went down to the station."

"Really? I didn't see her there that night."

Then again, it was three in morning by the time I left, and even if I had walked past her, I wouldn't have recognized the woman. I've done my best to avoid politicians and their campaigns.

"It may have been after you already left. I don't know the exact time, but she says she met with one of the detectives on the case and gave them the same statement she just gave me."

A glimmer of hope lights in my belly. "So, her story has stayed the same, and she was a good citizen and went to the police to give a report as soon as she was able to."

"Exactly."

"Then, the only real problem arises if there is a relationship between Danica and Enzo and the State were to find out about it?"

"Pretty much."

"Then we have to pray there isn't one or that they're both smart enough to keep it under wraps."

We end the call, and I drop back down onto the couch with a sigh.

It's good news.

I should be thrilled.

But it's impossible to celebrate this small victory when, as of now, I have nothing to help the client who is occupying my every waking thought and has made an appearance in a very hot dream after I left his place.

If I can't help him, I'm certain he'll haunt me forever, even worse than he already does.

8

FINLEY

The light knock on my office door pulls my attention away from the police reports I've buried myself in all afternoon to try to keep my mind from wandering to another client who seems impossible to forget. "Come in."

It swings open, and Charlotte steps in, carrying a large stack of papers in her right hand and a wadded-up tissue in her left. Her red, puffy, tear-soaked eyes meet mine, and my breath catches in my chest.

I shove to my feet and rush around the desk. "Oh, my God, are you okay? Is it the baby? More contractions?"

After all the excitement on Friday with her Braxton Hicks, Schwartz didn't even want her to come in today. But she insisted she needed to be here and be working to take her mind off how uncomfortable she is. Given how distressed she looks now, maybe it would have been better if she had agreed to take her maternity leave early.

Charlotte waves me off. "I'm fine. It's not that."

She waddles in and slowly lowers herself into one of the chairs facing my desk as I return to mine.

"What's wrong?"

Her gaze softens, and she holds up the stack of papers and waves them slightly in front of her. "Did you see what I emailed you a couple hours ago?"

I swallow thickly, averting my attention to unnecessarily shuffling the papers on my desk, and give a sharp nod. "Yes. Jude Lawson's medical records." I glance up at her. "I'm surprised you got them so fast. They usually take weeks to receive once we've made a request."

Charlotte nods. "Considering the circumstances of the case, I knew we had to get them quickly. So, I followed up on our emailed demand Friday morning and again this morning, and they were able to email them right away."

She must have really been up their asses to get them so quickly, but she's right about needing them fast. The sooner I can convince ADA Waters that Jude's injuries prevent him from being able to have executed those two men, the sooner I'll have the charges dropped and that man out of my life for good.

Her eyes drop to the stack again. "I've been reviewing them. Have you had a chance to take a look?"

I shake my head. "No."

Because I've been intentionally avoiding it and instead burying myself in anything else I can—currently discovery on a drunk and disorderly—so I won't have to think about the man who has insisted on occupying my dreams. If that sweaty, hot one I woke up from in the middle of the night last night is any indication, they won't be going away anytime soon.

Charlotte dabs her eyes again with the tissue. "Well, make sure you have a box of tissues ready when you do."

My chest tightens. "That bad?"

She sighs and sets the stack on the edge of my desk. "Fucking awful, Finley. This guy..." She takes a deep breath and rests her hands on her belly. "He lost his entire life. The amnesia and aphasia appear to be permanent. They drilled into his head and took out an entire section of his skull to relieve the swelling caused by his brain smashing around. He was in the hospital for months, trying to rehab and retrain his mind, trying to get back who he was before he finally signed out AMA."

"He signed out AMA?"

She nods. "The doctor's notes said he became frustrated with his lack of progress and decided he would rehabilitate himself at home."

"Shit."

Although it doesn't surprise me at all based on what I do know about the man.

"Yeah. I really think you should look at these sooner rather than later." Charlotte shakes her head. "I can't imagine any juror would be able to hear testimony about this and not only feel for the guy but also think it's impossible for him to have been able to carry out an assassination like they're accusing him of. It just isn't something people with the kind of brain damage he has are capable of."

I press my lips together to keep myself from revealing anything I've learned about him that I shouldn't know as his attorney and instead hold my hand out for the papers. "Give me the printed ones. I'll take a look at them since you already have a hard copy instead of looking at them on my computer."

She shifts forward in her chair with a grunt, and I reach across to take them from her.

"You can see I've tabbed a couple places I thought were especially important things. I think if this goes to trial, we're going to need to have an expert come in to testify about all this medical stuff."

"Agreed. Start looking for some experts on TBI, amnesia, and aphasia. Make a list for me so I can start contacting people."

"Got it."

"Thank you. I appreciate it."

She releases a little sigh, grabs the edge of the desk, and uses it to help hoist herself up from the chair with her other hand on her lower back.

"Are you sure you should be here? I mean, if reading these is making you burst into tears..."

Charlotte glowers at me. "That has nothing to do with the fact that I'm a hormonal mess and about to pop and everything to do with what that man's been through. You read them, and I challenge you not to cry."

"You know Schwartz is going to try to get you to go on leave early again if he sees you like this."

She swipes under her eyes and sucks in a deep breath. "And I'll tell him exactly what I'm telling you. I'm fine. Really." Waddling to the door, she glances back at me. "Don't forget the tissues."

Fucking hell.

Mouth is even getting to my paralegal, and she's never even *met* the man.

The door clicks shut behind Charlotte. I lean back in my chair and stare at the stack of medical records. She's right, of course. I need to review them as soon as possible and get a copy to ADA Waters. This is the type of information that could get this case dismissed short of trial. Exactly what could get Jude Lawson out of New York and out of my orbit.

My gut twists. Even though it's better for everyone if he isn't here, the thought of him leaving is somehow worse.

I nudge the police reports I was working on to the side and grab a pen to start taking notes on Jude Lawson's medical records. Within five minutes, my eyes begin to burn with unshed tears, and I clench my fist on the top of my desk, annoyed at how easily Charlotte knew what my reaction would be.

Dammit.

Charlotte was right; this is horrific.

No one should have to suffer through this. Losing who they are. The good memories with the bad. Their ability to interact with people on a basic level. No wonder he acts like he has a chip on his shoulder.

He's carrying around a massive one.

I've only seen him let down his guard once, for a few seconds while we were eating. He was calm, relaxed, carefree, just enjoying a meal with me while I kept talking to myself like he was responding.

He might have even been *happy* for those brief moments.

But it was gone just as fast.

Reading these, I wouldn't be surprised if I don't ever see it again.

MOUTH

THE HOSPITAL'S QUIET, dimly lit halls late at night carry the same smells and sounds that have haunted me for years.

Months in a place like this.

Being told things would get better.

People forcing me to try to remember things my mind had already lost.

Arguments with those who were supposed to be protecting me and helping me.

Anger and pain.

So much pain.

That antiseptic scent invades my lungs, and the longer I stand here, waiting for the signal, the stronger the migraine becomes—hammering at my skull like a sledgehammer intent on breaking it more than it already has been.

The soft squeaking of the nurses' shoes on the tile floors and the beeping and hissing of the various machines keeping people alive reach me through the pain.

But there's one person here who doesn't deserve to be breathing.

A spineless piece of shit...

When Parrish texted earlier tonight that Guthrie was awake and needed to be taken care of, an immense twisted conflict of anger and determination raced in my head.

This would have been a lot easier if he never woke up from the coma. If he had simply died and faded away into oblivion, the way he made the girl he bought disappear, but now, I get to do what I do best.

Well, second best.

Killing this asshole would be the ultimate vengeance for what he's done, but I understand Parrish's reasoning. If Guthrie dies, the guy they sent after him will be looking at murder charges—something they want to avoid in case it can ever be traced back to them. And since this guy sounds like a real moron, I wouldn't bet on that not happening.

I would have liked to avoid murder charges, too, but no such luck on my end.

Almost as a reminder of that fucked-up night, the migraine throbs again, brought on by all the reminders this place holds. Still young. Still new. But it's there, all the same, threatening to rush forward and knock me on my ass again.

Not tonight.

I just need to get this done and get back to the apartment. If I can do that, if I can complete this, then I will at least have one thing I didn't fuck up on this mission.

The blonde Parrish said would get me into Guthrie's room turns the corner and approaches where I wait near the stairwell door. She motions for me to follow her down the quiet hallway.

She glances back at me a couple of times as we make our way past the other ICU rooms but doesn't say anything. We pause outside a closed door, and she leans into me. "You have ten minutes before one of the other nurses comes to check on him."

I give her a sharp nod and step into the dark room lit only by the tiny lights on the machines beside his bed.

It would be so easy to end this now. To kill him and say *fuck you* to whoever Parrish is trying to protect. So damn easy it makes my hands flex to do it, to feel the life draining from him as I tighten them around his neck.

I approach slowly, examining the monster and utter douchebag. He looks so peaceful lying on the white pillow, eyes closed, chest rising and falling with his soft, silent breaths.

So damn easy to end them.

So damn unfair that he gets to keep living his life when his heinous actions have harmed so many others.

I stop beside his bed, pull the stack of notebook sheets from my back pocket, and shove my free hand over his mouth. His eyes fly open, and he scrambles, flailing his arms and legs and clawing at my wrist.

It's going to take a lot more than that to get me to release my grip, but I need him to calm down and pay attention. Even in the dim lighting, fear and panic soak his gaze, and I force my hand down harder again to get him to stop, holding up the first piece of paper I pre-wrote.

STOP FIGHTING ME.

His eyes widen as he reads it, and he gives me a sharp nod, relaxing slightly under my hold. I flip to the next page.

DON'T TALK.

Two words that speak volumes.

The tears that pool in his eyes make me want to move my hand down to his throat and tighten it there. But I can't. This man doesn't deserve to live, and everyone knows it, but the Knights are protecting whoever put him here, and it isn't my decision to make in this particular situation.

Any other time, he's exactly the kind of prick Reaper, Chaos, and I live to take down.

Perhaps another day.

Another place.

Preacher can easily keep tabs on this guy, and when the heat cools regarding whoever put him in here, I'll do what should be done now.

I show him the final page I wrote before I came up

here.

YOU TALK = YOU DIE!

This close to him, I can see the fear dilate his pupils. He gives me another sharp nod, and I pull my hand away from his mouth. If I can get to him here, I can get to him anywhere, and he knows it.

He won't fucking talk.

I make my way to the door and peek out the hallway to ensure the coast is clear. All remains quiet, and I slip out and casually move toward the stairwell, giving a sharp nod to the blonde where she sits at the charge desk at the end of the hall.

She doesn't acknowledge me but watches as I step through the door and hustle down the stairs. This time the swirl of vertigo only encroaches on the edges of my vision, but I grab the handrail anyway to ensure I'm not hit harder.

If this keeps happening every time I step out to handle a mission, I might as well go to prison because I'll be useless to Reaper and Chaos like this. Useless to all those people who come to us seeking justice and protection.

I crack my neck from side to side to clear the tension building there and pull out my phone to text Parrish. He'll want to know right away that it's done and off their plate.

It's done. He's not talking.

The three little dots that indicate he's replying pop up almost immediately. **FUCK YEAH! Thanks, man.**

I slip the phone into my back pocket and push out into the warm summer night air, inhaling a deep breath of it, hoping it might clear the headache I've been trying to fight off since I stepped into the hospital, but only one thing seems to do that.

The one thing I can't have.

9

FINLEY

Brent Matthews' smarmy face fills the television screen, still bruised and bandaged from the surgery he had to repair the broken orbital socket Enzo caused. Now that I know what Matthews did to his ex-wife, what Enzo did to *him* doesn't seem like nearly enough.

"Thank you all for being here. The support you've shown over the last week and a half has truly touched me. As most of you know, I was brutally attacked after my last fundraiser, and the recovery has not been an easy one."

I fight my gag reflex and roll my eyes.

Dramatic much?

The man—no doubt—had aides running around like little lemmings, completely at his beck and call the entire time he was laid up in the hospital. And what does he do the moment he gets released—rush straight to the press to figure out a way to milk the situation for everything he can before the election.

Absolute douchebag.

I'd give anything to push him aside on that podium and tell everyone gathered in front of him that he abuses women. Instead, I have to sit here in my office and listen to this horseshit.

"*But it is because of all your well wishes and my unbridled desire to serve this community that I will prevail. There's work to be done, and I will not let this unfortunate situation deter me from my quest to be District 11's next congressman.*"

The audience applauses, and Matthews pauses, slowly lifting a hand to his chest to appear moved by their claps.

Absolute total douchebag.

He holds up a hand to the crowd. "*Thank you!*" The clapping starts to die down. "*That being said, it is with a heavy heart that I announce I will be severing ties with Frankie's House. My hope is that the organization continues to help the community, especially our youth, but for personal reasons not attached to my campaign, I can no longer support the establishment.*"

I snort and shake my head. Frankly, I expected Matthews to flat-out say the man who assaulted him is connected to the charity. It's public record that Enzo was charged, and it's already made the newspapers. The only reason I can come up with that Matthews *isn't* calling him out is his fear of the Knights retaliating if he does.

Which is a legit concern.

"*I do not condone violence of any kind.*"

Except trying to strangle your ex-wife...

The pure hypocrisy of the statement makes me want to release Danica's statement to the press right now, but that won't do Enzo any good.

"*I stand for law and order and the wholesome values the neighborhoods I serve were built on. We will rise from this. Justice will be served, and on Election Day, the great people of Staten Island and Brooklyn will send me to Capitol Hill, knowing I have their best interests at heart. We will be a community that bands together. A community that lifts one another up. We will not knock each other down, and we will not turn a blind eye to violent crimes. The streets of our city have been filled with crime for too long. It's time to take a stand, and I hope you stand with me.*"

This entire dramatic show makes my stomach churn. It's a good thing I haven't had time to eat yet today, or my lunch might have ended up spewed across the files covering my desk.

Cheers and further applause pour from the crowd, reporters taking photos and calling out questions. Matthews doesn't respond to a single one. He stands at the podium, a plastered-on saccharine-sweet smile never moving from his lips, waving and eating it the fuck up.

Why wouldn't he?

The assault plays in his favor. It's a way to gain some sympathy votes while also beefing up his stance on violence and crime in the district.

You aren't getting my vote, fucker.

He wouldn't be getting any if people knew what Danica said happened. But as of right now, the police reports won't be released publicly. Unless the press manages to get someone to sneak them copies, they won't know Matthews' ex-wife said he assaulted her. And I'm banking on the fact that he will do anything to prevent those reports and the statement we have from ever going public.

Finally, his campaign manager steps to the podium. "*Mr. Matthews won't be taking any questions. Under his doctor's advisement, he will be heading home to take it easy for a couple of days. We'll see you next week on the campaign trail.*"

I shift my focus back to the files on my desk, mostly tuning out the continued questions being thrown by the reporters since he doesn't seem inclined to answer any.

"*Mr. Matthews, do you have any comment on your business partner's attack? Is there any correlation?*"

"*Mr. Matthews, what does this mean for your ex-wife? Will she still be involved with Frankie's House?*"

"*Does she still support your campaign?*"

"*What does she think about your girlfriend?*"

That question draws my eyes back to the TV. Matthews' manager tries to usher him from the podium, but he brushes the hand away.

His shrewd, intent gaze lands on someone in the crowd, and he steps back and adjusts the microphone. "*Danica and I will always support one another. She may no longer be my wife, but she's always been my anchor, and that shall remain true until the end of time.*"

Fucking hell.

My hand tightens to a fist around my pen, and I

shake my head. "You're in for a surprise when you find out about her statements, asshole."

He won't be happy to learn she came forward with what really happened that night and that she has no intent on backing whatever his version of events is in court—or with the press.

This could get very messy.

The shrill ring of my cell makes me drop my pen and reach for it.

Enzo.

One guess why he's calling...

I pull the phone to my ear and lean back in my chair. "Hey, Enzo."

"Did you see that circus Matthews just held outside the hospital?"

"Sure did."

"Am I allowed to say he's a total asshole?"

I chuckle and spin my chair to stare out the window. "You can say whatever you want as long as no one else is around to hear you. And, for the record, I agree—completely. He's going to milk this for all it's worth, even if everything he says is a fabrication."

"What about his little parting statement about Danica?"

"You have nothing to worry about. Not only did Danica go to the police the night of the incident and tell them exactly what you told me, but she also gave my private investigator a statement confirming it. She will testify that you were only protecting *her* and only *after* Matthews violently attacked her."

He clears his throat. "I knew she'd do the right thing, but…"

"But Brent Matthews holds a lot of power around here, and she might have felt pressured to back him despite what really happened?"

"Yeah."

"My investigator said she came across as very sincere and believable. That a jury will love her. That's *very* good for us. Matthews doesn't want this story getting out, so I'm going to have a little private conversation with the ADA handling your case and see if we can't make it go away without even having to go back to court again."

"You really think you can pull that off?"

I climb to my feet and walk over to the window, leaning my shoulder against it to look down at the bustling street. "You know I can't promise you anything, but if I were Matthews' attorney or campaign manager, I would want the statements from Danica buried so deeply that no one will ever get a whiff of it. I'll threaten to release her signed affidavit to the press and see where that gets us."

"Thank you, Ms. Banks. I appreciate it more than you could possibly know."

"Save your appreciation for when I get these charges dismissed."

"Deal."

He ends the call, and I slip my phone into my pocket and cross my arms over my chest. We have information that could destroy Matthews, but I still don't trust the Danica-Enzo situation. If he's hiding anything about their history or why he was there that night, it might come back to bite us in the ass in a way that we can never recover from.

I return to my desk, trying to forget about the press conference and the potential complications in Enzo's case, but my mind seems to only go in one direction—directly toward Jude Lawson.

What I read in his medical records keeps flashing in my head, reminding me constantly of what he's suffered and is currently going through. Being cooped up in that apartment can't help the situation, and he isn't the type to ever complain about being in pain.

Laura may not understand why I had to go check on him, but if she knew what I did, she would know why I have to go back.

MOUTH

THE MIGRAINE THAT started at the hospital hasn't abated, even with the litany of medications I've taken since last night. It's going to be a bad one, which means I need to take care of this before it fully settles in.

I can't have another incident like what happened with the Yankovich hit. I can't be caught in such a weak moment again or be so vulnerable, especially when, according to my ankle monitor, I'm sitting back at the apartment on the couch, watching television like a good little inmate.

But it's okay.

This won't take long.

The men sit at a table near the large front window of the restaurant, chatting, drinking, laughing, and groping the waitress each time she stops by to deliver their drinks and food.

Fucking assholes.

This late, the place is almost empty—free of innocent customers who could potentially get caught in the crossfire. It's the only reason I've waited this long to get rid of these fuckers tonight.

Fewer witnesses.

Fewer potential complications.

Otherwise, I would have smoked them hours ago when they arrived.

The waitress reappears with another tray of food, and the douchebag on the far right smacks her ass as she walks away. He laughs and waggles his dark eyebrows at his friends while the girl winces and casts an angry look back at him. No one at the table can see her reaction, but I don't miss it, watching through my scope.

A sharp pang in my chest briefly makes the migraine pain disappear, replacing it with something far worse. It's impossible not to feel for her, not to want to storm over there and beat those men to death and torture them the way they do these women. To let her see there are people out there who care about what happens to her and are willing to take action against those who think they're untouchable.

She deserves to know not all men are like these guys

—something she likely hasn't ever experienced. Chances are good that she was brought over with their trafficking business. It certainly wouldn't surprise me if they kept a few for themselves and put them to work at their own establishments since these fuckers have no souls.

But what they do have are heads and chests—things I can hit with a fucking bullet. The ones loaded in my rifle right now have their names on them.

I've spent enough time watching them, waiting for the perfect opportunity. It's time to finally act. To end what I started when I came to New York, what Reaper entrusted me with.

All six of the men Preacher identified have gathered here tonight. They've worked together to ruin lives, and now, they'll die together.

Any of Yankovich's men who managed to live through what we did last year and somehow escape what I'm about to do tonight will be left without their organization. They'll scatter and hopefully disappear into oblivion. If they don't...I can always come back.

We'll never stop protecting the innocent any way we can, and if that means a thousand trips to hunt down these pieces of shit, so be it.

Now.

The waitress has safely walked away, and I'm in the clear. I fire off the shots in quick succession. They shatter the glass of the front window and impact each of the men so fast that no one knows what's happening.

All of them crumble in their seats, two of them tumbling to the floor.

A sense of accomplishment swells in my chest as I rise to my feet, police my brass, and tear down my rifle to put it into the case. Even though it's only been just over a week, it felt like this was a long time coming. And in a way, it was, since those men slipped through our grasp when we took out the bulk of the organization.

Mission accomplished.

I throw the rifle case over my shoulder and hustle down the steps from the third floor of the building across the street. Memories of the night I took out their boss come swirling back. Of the vertigo on the steps. My stomach revolting. The police snapping the cuffs on my wrists while I wretched.

Shaking my head, I take the final flight.

It's not happening tonight.

I'm getting home before it hits.

Through sheer willpower, I fight the pain and casually stroll to my car the next block over. I drive away slowly, going exactly two miles per hour over the speed limit. Nothing an officer would ever notice or pull me over for.

Getting caught outside the apartment when I'm supposed to be on house arrest would be bad enough, but with a rifle in the car and six bodies back at that restaurant, there wouldn't be any way to escape going to prison.

My vision starts to blur as the tension in my head mounts. I tighten my grip on the wheel and shake my head slightly, narrowing my eyes to try to ensure I keep a good view of the road in front of me.

Reaper was so confident I could handle this on my own, and I almost fucked it up tonight. Again. If I'd been out there another half an hour more, I might have found myself in the exact same position with the way the agony is building.

I pull my car up a block from the apartment, grab my rifle case, and slowly make my way toward the front door of my building, the sidewalk blurring under my feet.

"Ahem."

Someone clears their throat, and I lift my head, knowing exactly who it is without even having to look.

Finley leans next to the entrance to my building, a scowl on her perfect, pink, bow lips, eyes and jaw hard. She glowers at me and pushes off the wall. "Where the hell were you?" Her eyes dart down to the case in my hand and widen. She whips her head side to side, ensuring no one is around us. "Is that what I fucking *think* it is?"

Fuck.

Instead of answering my very annoyed attorney, I step around her, put my key in the lock, twist it, and open the door.

She grabs my arm, tightening her hand as much as she can around my bicep. "Answer me, Mouth. You can't just walk away and pretend I didn't just see what I think I saw."

I can certainly try.

This is a conversation I would rather avoid entirely.

I continue to ignore her, press the button for the

elevator, and squeeze my eyes closed against the threatening vertigo, inhaling deeply.

That crisp citrus-mint scent she always seems to have invades my breath, and the tiniest bit of tension releases from my head.

Fuck.

The elevator door dings and slides open, and I step inside, knowing she'll follow directly behind me. There's no shaking her tonight. There's no coming up with some excuse or explanation. She knows what I carry in my hand and what I was doing with it—there's no way around that.

Finley steps into the car, standing directly in front of me, chest almost touching mine. "*Answer* me, Mouth. None of this silent bullshit with me tonight." She glances down at my ankle as we move up. "Where the hell is your ankle monitor?"

I lock my eyes with hers, and the elevator jerks to a stop on my floor. The doors slide open, and I step around her and out to unlock my place. She rushes into the apartment behind me and slams the door.

The sound reverberates through the room and off the high ceilings. I glance over my shoulder at her and find her standing with her hands propped on her hips, a wild, angry blush flooding her cheeks.

"I swear to fucking Christ, Mouth, if you don't answer me—"

It's better if I don't, so I point to the counter where the ankle monitor flashes green against the granite—

exactly where it has sat every time I've left the condo to do recon on the Russians since Preacher figured it out.

She stalks over and grabs it. "You rigged your ankle monitor?"

I shake my head.

Her lips twist into a scowl, and she throws up her hands. "Well, maybe not *you* personally, but it seems you have resources who are pretty fucking smart." She sets it back on the counter with a scowl at me. "Unlike you, apparently."

True statement.

It was stupid to think I could ever be in the same room as this woman and control the way my body reacted to her. In the no more than one minute we were in that elevator together, my migraine already started to ease while the ache migrated to between my fucking legs.

I move over to the closet and hide the gun behind the few clothes I have hanging there before turning back to her.

Finley shakes her head, sending her long, silky brunette hair flying wildly around her face. "What the hell am I supposed to do with you, Mr. Lawson? I now have knowledge that you've violated your bond by tampering with your ankle monitor, leaving your residence, and..." She stops short of saying what's obvious, but her eyes dart toward the closet. "I know what you did that night with Yankovich. I can only presume it was the same thing you were doing tonight?"

That must be a rhetorical question. She can't

possibly want me to answer her and explain I just killed half a dozen men.

I raise an eyebrow but don't answer.

"Jesus, Mouth." She shoves her hands back through her hair and stalks toward me, stopping a few feet away. "Do you have any idea the position you've put me in? How much trouble this can cause for both of us?"

10

FINLEY

This man is infuriating.

He stands mere feet from me, staring into my eyes and watching me as if I haven't just confronted him about murdering people, about violating his bond, about the fact that he just walked in here carrying a goddamn rifle case.

"How long before I get a call from the DA's office saying that more members of Yankovich's crew were killed tonight?" I tap my foot and raise an eyebrow at him. "Tomorrow?"

He takes a step closer, his imposing form starting to loom over me.

This man just went out and killed someone. Maybe multiple someones. I have no doubt about that. Yet, here I am with him. In his goddamn apartment. Standing so close that I can smell the night air on him mingling with gunpowder and leather and a strong masculine scent that makes my entire body clench.

He offers a shrug to my question and inhales deeply, closing his eyes.

"What the hell are you doing?"

His lids slowly flutter open, his body relaxing slightly, but he still doesn't say anything.

"I'm not playing this game tonight, Mouth. I know you can talk, so *fucking talk*. I can't be your lawyer if you're going to do this. I can't be involved in this. I can't be involved with—"

The word "you" almost slips out of my mouth, but instead, I bite it back, unwilling to voice what's been rattling around in my head since the moment I met this man.

The corner of his lip twitches, almost like he knew what I was going to say. He takes another step closer— this time, close enough that the heat radiating off his body seeps into my skin.

"Please, Mouth. I need to know what we're looking at. I need to know what to say when I get a call from the DA about this because they're going to try to pin it to you if whatever you just did is in any way connected to the murders you're already charged with. They're going to know, and they're going to come for *you*."

He inclines his head toward the counter, where the piece of technology that's supposed to keep him here sits, almost taunting me with its uselessness. "B-b-but I was h-h-here the whole n-n-night."

I fist my hands at my sides. "What if someone saw you? A witness?"

Mouth shakes his head. "N-n-no one saw m-m-me."

"You have to be out of your ever-loving mind." I release a heavy sigh, my frustration making it difficult to even form words. "You know why I came here tonight?"

He smirks, and I practically growl at him.

"I was *worried* about you. About your being here alone, with no support system, trapped inside an apartment that isn't even your home. And you go and do this, making me look like a total asshole for ever being concerned."

Mouth appears unmoved by my concern. His blue eyes spark with something that definitely isn't anger or worry. He offers a casual shrug again and finally steps so close that his chest brushes against mine. "There isn't a-a-anything to w-w-worry about. I'm g-g-good at my j-j-job, Ms. Banks."

"And what is your *job*?" I raise an eyebrow at him, refusing to back down or retreat even in his powerful presence.

He smirks again. "You kn-kn-know. I w-w-work for a p-p-private security c-c-company."

I scowl at him. "Which is a front for what? Seems to me like you're a fucking mercenary."

A killer.

Mouth offers a casual shrug as if accusing him of that doesn't mean anything.

As expected, he doesn't respond.

"What the hell am I supposed to do with you, Mr.

Lawson? Just let you continue to run around killing people while you're supposed to be on bond for killing people?"

The continued silence claws at my patience, and I shake my head, throwing up my hands. "Fucking *talk* to me."

"W-w-what do you want me to s-s-say?"

"Anything? Nothing? Fuck. I don't know. I just want you to—"

My words get swallowed by his lips crashing against mine, and despite my surprise at the sudden kiss, I don't push him away.

I should.

He's my client.

He's dangerous.

He's a *killer.*

But I don't push him away. I don't run. I can't.

I issue a little moan as my body responds to his, molding myself to his hard, firm chest. His mouth moves against mine eagerly, as if all this arguing has built up some sort of soul-crushing need instead of making him want to throw me out of here like he should.

Mouth's cock hardens between us, pinned against my belly, and my pussy clenches at the thought of having that between my legs. So much strength. So much power. So much turmoil all wrapped up into one man.

His tongue sweeps against mine, seeking, longing, stroking, demanding, and I cling to his T-shirt to keep my shaking legs from giving out under me.

Fuck. What the hell am I doing?

I push away from him and stagger back, hand over my mouth, my heart thundering against my chest and heated blood rushing in my ears—my entire body hot and primed and ready for something that can never happen.

"What the hell am I doing?" I say it out loud this time like I'm going to get some sort of answer, as if Mouth is actually going to give me one.

He takes another step toward me and dips his head to meet my eyes, concern and heat lingering in his gaze.

I shake my head to try to dispel the fuzziness over-taking my brain. "We can't do this. We can't. I could lose my license for getting involved with a client. Fuck...even for just being here in a position like this. I...shit. I should know better."

Squeezing my eyes closed, I fist my hands at my sides to keep myself from reaching out for the hard, warm body directly in front of me.

His strong, calloused palm captures my cheek and tilts my face up to his. I let my eyes open to meet his, and all I want is to close the distance between us. To feel his lips on mine again.

No.

I back away, watching his hand fall to his side. "I can't."

This is wrong. On so many levels.

Wrong for me.

Wrong for him.

Just *wrong.*

I rush to the door, throw it open, and race to the stairwell, afraid that if I wait for the elevator, he'll come after me.

Fuck. Who am I kidding?

That man is likely faster and stronger than anyone I've ever met. If he really wanted to make me stay, he'd already be on me, forcing me to.

And as much as I don't want to admit it, a massive part of me wishes he would do just that.

MOUTH

"Fuck!"

I run my hands through my hair, stalk over to the open door Finley just ran out of, and slam it shut, the sound vibrating through my chest with my pent-up frustration.

Her minty scent that seems to alleviate the pain in my head and in my fucking soul still permeates the air, mocking me with what was just in my grasp but I can never truly have.

Fucking hell.

That woman masquerades as a law-abiding, upstanding attorney, but really, she's a fucking menace. An exasperating temptress sent to drive me insane and twist me up in ways I never could have imagined. To make me question everything I'm doing and everything I have done. To make me want something I *know* I can never have for too many reasons to count.

And she's right, of course.

She's my lawyer, and getting involved with her, kissing her, even *thinking* about it is as fucking inappropriate a position as I can put her in. It could destroy her career. Her life. End her ability to do the thing she loves and is so damn good at.

All because my dick decided to come to life after four years of snoozing and shriveling from disuse. With the taste of her still on my lips, that scent hanging in the air, my painfully hard cock twitches against the front of my pants.

Fuck. Fuck. Fuck.

This went too far.

I went too far.

It would be easy to blame it on being amped up after what I did tonight, or on the migraine, on both of those things combined, but it's so much more than that—and that's what makes it so dangerous.

Neither of us can afford the kind of complications this brings.

It can't happen.

My dick thinks otherwise, though, so I head to the bathroom, crank on the shower as hot as it'll go, strip, and step under the spray while it's still icy cold. Maybe the chill of the water will help cool my libido and convince my body it's not gonna fucking happen. That I won't feel her warm cunt wrapped around it tonight, that I won't come down her pretty throat or deep inside her.

Goddammit!

My cock doesn't go down, even with the icy water

pelting it and my best efforts to enforce the reality of our situation. There's only one way this is going to fucking resolve.

I grit my teeth and take my length in my hand, a low groan rumbling in my chest at the relief the first stroke brings. The water begins to warm, hitting my already heated skin, and I grip myself tightly, remembering the way she plastered her body to mine.

Her breasts pushing against my chest.

Her hands clinging to my T-shirt.

That tiny little moan that came out of her throat when my lips hit hers.

Fucking Christ, that woman...

I can't remember what it was like to be with someone in that way.

To argue with her.

To hold her.

To kiss her.

To fuck her.

To completely lose myself in another person who wants to be with me.

All I ever see are flashes. Brief moments of the past that never linger long or give me any sense of context. The only thing I have to picture with my hard cock in my hand is that fiery brunette who holds my life in her small, soft ones.

Every stroke tightens my body more, and I move faster, slamming my free palm to the tile and letting my head fall forward, the now-scalding water hitting the back of my head and neck and flowing down over my shoulders. The tension that's been building since the moment my eyes first landed on Finley in that police station struggles to release, fighting against the part of me that knows how fucking *wrong* this is. How wrong I am for *her*.

All kinds of wrong.

I'm a killer, a man who operates on the wrong side of the law, and she's someone who has built a life and career on ensuring it's upheld. Her passion for her clients and job shines in everything she does. And it shows me how determined she will continue to be to keep a wall up between us, to protect herself from what it would mean for her career.

And it's for the best.

Even if no woman has ever affected me like that—at least, not one I can remember. She's the first one in almost five years who doesn't look at me with pity. Who doesn't look at me like something to be fixed or nursed back to health. She knows exactly what I am and what I do, saw evidence of it tonight. Yet, she still kissed me back. She still wanted it and needed it as much as I did in that moment.

One that can never be repeated.

I stroke harder and faster, imagining her lean but curvy frame spread out under me as I drive into her welcoming heat over and over again, desperately trying to find something I haven't been able to in so fucking long that I forgot what it even feels like.

My orgasm builds quickly. The tingling at the base of

my spine surging through my body until my cock hardens even more in my grip.

Fuck.

My cum spurts out over my hand and onto the tile, the rush of water pounding around me, washing it down the drain at my feet. If only it were that easy to wash away my feelings for that woman, the way she affects my mind, body, and soul. It won't be that easy, though. Nothing in my life ever is or ever will be again.

It can't be. I don't deserve it to be, and the big man upstairs has made that abundantly clear.

My future is destined to be filled with more pain, more struggles, more unfulfilled dreams like being with Finley.

I stand motionless with my hand firmly wrapped around my still-hard cock, the release not enough to cure my desire for her.

How could I ever think it would be?

She's as addictive as she is fierce.

As controlled as she is passionate.

As beautiful as she is dangerous.

When Reaper sent me here, I thought this mission was going to be a problem because of my fucked-up head, but it turns out it's Finley Banks who is the problem. Because I don't know if there's any way I can stop myself from doing again what I did tonight, the next time I see her any more than I can stop my trigger finger when I see someone who deserves it.

11

MOUTH

The high afternoon sun beats down overhead as I light up my cigarette and settle into my usual spot on the balcony to wallow in my misery over what happened last night.

That wasn't fair to Finley, and I never should have put her in that position. I certainly shouldn't have jerked off, fantasizing about her after she left.

It only makes the reality of the impossibility of it worse. It's only going to make things harder going forward for us.

I take a long drag, and my phone lights up with an incoming text.

Chaos: Open up, asshole.

What the hell?

A hard knock sounds at the door, and I snuff out my cigarette, climb inside, and make my way over to the door. I throw it open and barely have time to register Chaos' grin before Avery throws herself at me.

"Mouth!"

I catch her small frame and hug her tightly as Chaos chuckles and brushes past us into the apartment.

He glances back. "Our flight home came through LaGuardia, so we thought we'd stop and say hello before heading back home."

Avery pulls back from our embrace and smiles at me. "You look good. A lot better than I thought you would, considering the circumstances."

I smirk at her back-handed compliment and press a kiss to her forehead as she slides out of my arms.

Chaos scowls at me. "Hey, keep your lips off my wife."

I grin at him and mouth, "Your *wife*."

He just smiles back.

There was a time not that long ago when none of us thought this could ever happen. That Kalen and Avery would never find their way back to each other. Seeing them like this—happy and tan from lying in the sun in Mexico for their literal second honeymoon—I can't help but feel like I'm staring at a miracle.

Chaos claps me on the shoulder, and we walk deeper into the apartment as Avery scans it.

Her jaw drops. "Wow, this place is really nice. Are you going to keep it once your case is resolved?"

I glance at Chaos.

How much does she know?

Without having to voice the question, Chaos responds to her for me.

"I don't think anyone has any intention of keeping this place, Avery."

She laughs and spins around with her arms out wide. "Why not? It's great. We could use it when we come to the city."

Chaos and I exchange a look. He shakes his head and pulls his wife into his arms. "There isn't any reason for any of us to be in New York once Mouth can come home."

Yet, I wish there were. I wish Finley could be that reason. But that's impossible. And after everything that went down since I arrived in New York, I don't have any desire to ever come back unless absolutely required to by a job. Even then, I'll do my best to send Reaper or Chaos without me. The Big Apple has turned sour for me—for a lot of reasons. The least of which is the beautiful woman I can never have.

Pushing away those thoughts, I lead Avery and Chaos into the kitchen and grab each of us a beer.

Chaos accepts his and motions toward the open window to the fire escape. "Hey, babe, Mouth and I need to talk about some stuff. You hang out in here, okay?"

She takes a sip of her beer, leaning against the counter, and offers a tight smile that tells me she knows we're going to be discussing something she probably wouldn't like.

After what went down only a few months ago, Avery knows there are some things she'll never be privy to. She isn't like Viktoria. She wasn't a cop or in any way a part of this life, and there isn't any reason to drag her into it by exposing her to information she shouldn't know.

Chaos follows me out the window and takes my seat on the step, leaving me to stand against the railing. He glances through the window to ensure she isn't looking or listening and takes a sip of his beer. "Avery wanted to stop to say hi and see how you're doing, but I wanted to make sure you don't need me to stay and help you with the Russians."

I shake my head and mouth, "*It's done.*"

His dark eyebrows rise. "Already?"

The genuine shock in his question slices at my heart more than maybe anything else ever has. There was a time when he never would have questioned my ability to handle this on my own, a time when he and Reaper and the rest of the team relied on me to be unshakably accurate and lethal. The fact that he questions it now is just another reminder of no longer being that person.

Almost as if he can read my thoughts, he winces. "Shit, I didn't mean it like that. It's just that I talked to Reaper yesterday, and he said you were still working on it."

I set down my beer and pull out my notebook.

Got the six Preacher found last night.

He holds up his beer bottle. "Nice job." His eyes dart down to the monitor on my ankle. "How long are you going to be attached to that thing and stuck here?"

I release a heavy sigh and rub my neck before I write my response.

Don't know. However long it takes my attorney to resolve this. If we end up having to go to trial, it could be months or maybe even a year.

Chaos narrows his eyes on me. "Is your lawyer good? Does he know what he's doing?"

I stiffen at the question, and the memory of her lips moving with mine flashes to the front of my brain.

She. And she definitely knows what she's doing.

She's a real pit bull.

He chuckles. "I guess she'd have to be if Parrish trusts her."

I nod and retrieve my beer to take another long drink. The last thing I want to be discussing with Chaos is Finley. He knows me too well, actually, better than I know myself since I can't remember any of the years we spent together before my injury.

Chaos can read me like an open book, and he narrows his gaze on me now. "Something going on with your attorney, Mouth?"

Shifting my stance, I avoid looking directly at him and shake my head.

He watches me for a minute, sipping his beer, then finally averts his gaze down to his feet. "I'm sorry I wasn't here to help you with all this. You wouldn't be in this position if I—"

"N-n-no."

He jerks his head up and looks at me, his brow furrowed. It's the first time he's heard my voice in four years, the only time I've wanted to say something badly enough that it compelled me to do it with actual spoken words instead of writing it to him. But I can't bear hearing myself anymore.

This isn't your fault. Just bad timing with one of my migraines.

His gaze softens as he examines me, searching for an answer to a question he hasn't even asked yet. "Are they getting any better?"

I clench my jaw and shake my head.

Not unless I'm with Finley

Chaos takes another drink, looking out at the part of the city we can see from the fire escape. "You're sure you're good here?"

We've waited things out in worse places, haven't we?

He barks out a laugh and rises to his feet, clapping his hand on my shoulder. "A lot fucking worse. But Reaper and I are both here for you, even if we're not here." He motions around us. "You know we're only a text away and we'll be here in two hours."

I nod my understanding, and he steps through the

window. If we leave Avery alone in there any longer, she's going to get restless. I follow him in to find Avery looking in the fridge.

"I was checking to see if you had something I could make us if we stay for lunch, but you don't have much in here. What do you eat?"

I grin at her, set my beer on the counter, and grab my notebook.

Takeout.

She reads it and scowls. "That sounds healthy."

I know a great meatball place we can order from.

She raises an eyebrow. "Meatballs?"

Trust me. They'll leave you craving more.

Just like my damn attorney has.

FINLEY

STARING AT MY UNEATEN LUNCH, I drum my fingers on my desk and finally grab my phone to make the call I've been waiting to initiate until I had given my opponent some time to consider his position on my client—while I consider my own position as it relates to him in a whole other way.

ADA Waters picks up the phone on the third ring and with an annoyed sigh. "Ms. Banks, there can be only one reason you're calling me during my lunch hour when you know I'll be out of court and at my desk. You want to ruin my damn day."

I chuckle and lean back in my office chair, letting my head drop against the headrest, picturing Jon with his sack lunch spread out across his desk piled high with case files. "Well, I think it's time we had a discussion about Mr. Lawson's case, especially now that I've reviewed all the police reports and his medical records."

The deep dive I did on the medical records rattled me, but after seeing them *and* the police reports, they've firmly convinced me that no juror will ever convict Jude Lawson of these homicides. His injuries and apparent disability are too severe, and this crime was far too meticulous and perfectly executed to have been done by a man who was so ill when the police found him that he literally vomited.

"What is that you think we have to discuss, Ms. Banks?"

He wants to play hard to get, and I understand it. It's his job to put criminals away, and that's how he sees Mouth. That assessment might not be wrong, but it isn't about what the DA prosecuting the case thinks and sees; it's about what he can convince a jury of.

"Oh, come on now, Jon. You and I have both been

doing this for a long time, and you know as well as I do that there's no way you can prove this case to a jury."

"That's a pretty hard stance you're taking."

Which has absolutely nothing to do with my attraction to the client.

"You don't have anything, Jon, except the testimony of a drug-addicted homeless man with a rap sheet two miles long who you might not be able to find or who may be dead by the time we go to trial. And he didn't even see my client *do* anything, just heard what he *believed* to be gunshots before the cops *happened* to find my client at the building. That's weak, Jon, and you know it."

"And just what was Mr. Lawson doing in that building, let alone at that time of night, Ms. Banks?"

"That's irrelevant."

He barks out a laugh. "It is very relevant, and *you* know it. We have a strong circumstantial case here. Who else is going to be able to take two shots like that, Ms. Banks, except a former member of the military, one who, I'm sure if I dug deep enough, would turn out to be trained as a sniper? You cannot tell me that man didn't do this."

I can't, but that isn't the question that is making us do all this work. And there is no way I'm going to confirm that Jon's right about the sniper training. The information Reaper gave me on Mouth's background is safely locked away in my head until I can get some sort of confirmation in writing from the government. Given his service record and what he did, those written reports are sure to be very lean on details—which is ideal for us from a case standpoint.

"You have no evidence that he *did*. You have no weapon. You have no gunpowder residue on his hands. You have nothing but a speculation that because he was in that building around the time the kill shots were taken, he must have been the one who took those shots."

"No one else was in the building."

"According to the reports, it took the police three minutes to get there after the report of shots being heard. That's a lot of time for someone to flee a scene."

Unless they're suffering from a debilitating migraine that prevents them from getting away.

I let ADA Waters ponder my words for a few minutes before I finally release a long sigh. "Come on, Jon. Why are we wasting time and the State's money on this when we both know you can't prove this beyond a reasonable doubt?"

"I think we can."

Good God, this man doesn't want to see the writing on the wall.

It's time I stick his face in it.

"I sent you a copy of Mr. Lawson's medical records. Did you review them?"

He clears his throat uncomfortably. "I skimmed them."

"And you really want a jury hearing about how Mr. Lawson was so damaged by his service that he has almost no solid memories of his life? That he has moments of confusion and excruciating migraines? That he, in fact, had one that made him throw up that night in front of officers? That perhaps he was in one of these confused states and happened to just wander into the abandoned building at the wrong time? All I need is one juror for a mistrial, Jon. *One.* You need all twelve to unanimously agree that he did this beyond a reasonable doubt, and you're not going to get them because there is all kinds of doubt in this case."

He's silent for a moment, likely because steam is shooting out of his ears, knowing I'm right. "I can't just let this go, Ms. Banks. He murdered two people."

"Allegedly." At this point, it's still important to emphasize that fact. "Why are you pushing this so hard? It's not like the victims here were anyone society is going to miss."

"That's exactly my point, Finley. I can't have vigilantes running around the city, killing whoever they feel like, acting as judge, jury, and executioner. We have a legal system for a reason. Did you know six other associates of Maksim Yankovich were hit two nights ago? It makes me wonder if your client has an accomplice."

His words sink in slowly.

Vigilantes.

Oh, my God.

That's what this is...

Jude Lawson never struck me as the cold-blooded killer type. Because he's not. I assumed he was acting on behalf of some rival of the Russians, some other group who hired him as a mercenary to remove the men standing in their way. But I had it all wrong. He took them out because they're *bad fucking men*. Men who likely would find a way to avoid ever having anything pinned on them. Men who would never go to prison or ever pay for their crimes.

He's a vigilante.

And that somehow makes things even worse.

"Review his records in detail, Jon, and really consider if you were a juror what you would think if you saw a decorated war hero with all sorts of physical and mental limitations because of his exemplary service, sitting there next to me, accused of committing a calculated crime that took precision he can't possibly execute anymore. Really think about whether you want to put your neck out there so publicly, to lose so badly, and then, call me so we can get this thing resolved and my client can go back to Baltimore."

As far away from me as possible. Before I do something stupid again with the man who is here for a purpose, one founded on the belief that he's doing the right thing.

He may be a killer, but he's one with a conscience.

And that changes everything.

12

MOUTH

Darkness starts to fall outside, and the door buzzer sounds in the apartment. Almost immediately, my heart climbs into my throat...

Finley.

I don't know how I know, but I do. Almost like I can sense her presence even from four stories down on the street.

What the hell is she doing back here after the way things ended the other night?

She should have stayed away. I thought she would revert to text messages and one-sided phone calls before she'd ever set foot in the same room alone with me again.

But I was wrong.

I could let it continue to buzz, let her believe I'm out

again, doing something I shouldn't be—according to her —but instead, I make my way over and press the button to let her in.

I'm part masochist and part selfish bastard. It's fucking torture being so close to her and not being able to have her, but it's also the most relief I get from the pain plaguing my body.

Something about her, about being around her, somehow releases the tension she also produces. It should make things worse, but that minty, crisp, fresh scent she carries everywhere with her somehow tames the raging damaged nerves in my head. She calms them as she simultaneously drives me insane.

I unlock the door and open it, leaning against the jamb to wait for her to come up in the elevator. Each second it takes seems to drag on, and I shift slightly, eyes locked on the metal contraption bringing her to me—the source of my turmoil and my potential salvation.

It dings, and I freeze, waiting for the doors to slide open. Her green eyes meet mine, and she steps out in the hallway and stops just in front of me.

"W-w-what are you doing here?"

A light blush spreads across her cheeks, but she doesn't look away. "I talked with the DA on your case today, and we need to have a little chat."

About the case or about what happened the other night?

I don't ask. I just follow her in and close the door behind us, throwing the deadbolt. This time, if she tries to run away, she'll have to really want to.

She stops in the middle of the open living room and

turns to face me. "I sent the ADA handling your case a copy of your medical records."

My entire body stiffens, my jaw tightening. "D-d-did you r-r-read them?"

Confusion furrows her brow. "Yes, of course. I had to know what I was sending him, had to know what was in them that might help our case."

I fist my hands at my sides, anger tightening in my chest. "Y-y-you n-n-never told me y-y-you would r-r-read them."

She pauses for a moment, her eyes widening slightly. "I had to, Mouth. I have to know everything about you. If I'm going to defend this case, if this thing makes it to trial, we're going to have to get a jury to understand your situation."

"M-m-my *si-si-situation*?"

What the hell is that supposed to mean?

Finley winces slightly. "I'm sorry. That didn't come out right."

"Th-th-that's what I h-h-have? A *si-si-situation*?"

"Shit." She pushes her hand back through her hair, her exhaustion and frustration lining her face. "Really, that's not what I meant. You saw how the judge reacted during your arraignment when I told him your history and your medical condition. That's the type of information that's going to be invaluable with both the ADA and the jury." Her green eyes connect with mine, begging me to understand. "You're a goddamn war hero who is now permanently disabled."

I flinch at the word, and her gaze immediately softens.

"Mouth—"

"P-p-please d-d-don't. Just s-s-stop. I don't w-w-want your f-f-fucking pity."

Her lips twist. "That's what you think? That I *pity* you?" Finley steps closer to me—this time, the anger all hers. She scoffs and releases a sardonic laugh. "I don't *pity* you, Mouth. I'm in *awe* of you and what you've been able to accomplish. What you've done in your life. What you're still *capable* of doing."

"You're n-n-not afraid of m-m-me?"

I take another step closer to her even though my own fear of being rejected again screams for me to retreat. To give her space. To walk back to that door, unlock it, throw it open, and *ensure* she leaves. But I force myself to keep moving until I'm standing in front of her, so close I could reach out and drag her up against me in a split second.

Finley stares up at me, her eyes clear of any fear. "I know what you can do. I know what you did the other night. I know what you're doing when you're supposed to be sitting here."

I fight a grin.

She finally figured it out.

"Whatever happened to you out on that deployment, whatever may be messed up in your head, it didn't change who you are. And I'm not afraid of you because, deep down, I believe you think you're doing the right thing."

The right thing right now would be for her to walk away. For her to run out of here as fast as her feet can carry her back to her place. Back to safety. Somewhere my tainted hands can't reach her. Somewhere she can find a man who will give her everything she deserves. Who isn't broken and damaged and on the verge of potentially going to prison for the rest of his life.

She takes a tentative half-step toward me. "If you think that what happened the other night was because I *pity* you, then you have it all wrong. I can't explain it, can't figure out why I'm so drawn to you. Why I can't stay away when I know I should." She shakes her head. "I don't know what it is, but I do know what it *isn't*. And it isn't pity. I could *never ever* pity you."

Those words reach deep inside me, to a part I thought had died along with the memories of the life I had before. The memories I fought so hard to get back but only return in painful flashes I can't understand.

Heat ripples across my skin, making it feel too tight, this condo suddenly too small to hold Finley and me and everything building between us.

"But you have to understand. This"—she motions between us—"this is far more dangerous than anything you do."

"L-l-leave."

I barely manage to get the word out between gritted teeth that don't want me to say it.

Finley keeps her gaze locked with mine. "I already know I should leave."

She takes a slow step toward the door, almost like she's waiting for me to object to the move.

I reach out and grab her shoulder, stopping her in place. "B-b-but you're n-n-not g-g-going to."

Her shoulders sag, almost as if in resignation, and she slowly turns to face me.

"Y-y-you could h-have called m-m-me to tell me about t-t-the c-c-call with the DA. E-e-especially after wh-wh-what happened the other n-n-night. But you di-di-didn't."

Because despite what the consequences may be, Finley is as drawn to me as I am to her. A force so strong, neither of us can deny it.

I tug her toward me, and she sags into my arms as I sweep my lips over hers. A tiny moan climbs up her throat, and she molds herself to me like she can't get close enough.

Her arms tighten around my neck. "Jude, please."

No one calls me Jude—at least, not that I can remember. Maybe Mom and Dad and Abigail and Michaela when I was a kid, but they're long gone from my life, along with any friends I've forced away after I couldn't remember them and fought their efforts to try to jog my memory. The only ones left call me Mouth because that's what I always was to them—the mouthy sniper who cracked jokes at the most inappropriate times and never shut up.

Hearing it from her lips instead of the nickname sends an inferno of need blazing through my veins.

Finley doesn't know Mouth, doesn't know who I was

when I got that nickname or why it was so damn fitting. She only knows who and what I am now—the shattered man with no past and an uncertain future.

Yet, she wants to be here. She wants *this*. Wants *me*.

I grab her hips and lift her small frame easily. She wraps her legs around my waist, aligning her core against my hardening cock and rolling her body, grinding down against me.

Fuck.

It's been so long since anyone has touched me, since I've felt a warm body molded to mine, seeking and desperate the way I am. Her tongue glides along mine, and I groan into her mouth as I consume her, content to take everything she is willing to give me because I have nothing to offer her.

Anything I had and everything I was disappeared with my old memories. But all she seems to want is this moment.

The only thing I *can* give her.

I walk to the bed, kissing her, clutching to her tightly, afraid if I loosen my grip, she might run for the door again, but she clings to me in a way I'm not sure any woman ever has.

All of it is new and exhilarating. Almost like it's my first time because, for all intents and purposes, it is. I don't remember what it's like to be with a woman, to have her under me and be inside her. But my body seems to know what to do, what it and she wants.

My shins hit the mattress, and I slowly lower her down onto it, tearing my lips from hers to skim them across her cheek, down her neck, and to the exposed *V* of cleavage in her white blouse.

Her chest heaves with heavy breaths, and I slide my fingers under the buttons and rip sideways, sending them flying across the room. Finley issues a sharp gasp at the destruction of her shirt, but the heat intensifies in her gaze as I tug down the cups of her pale-pink bra, exposing the mounds of flesh and hard nipples.

My mouth waters to taste them, to taste *her*, to devour every inch of her luscious body. She runs her fingers through my hair, scratching at my scalp and sending goosebumps over my skin. I duck my head and suck one taut peak between my lips. Her entire body arches off the bed against me, her legs tightening around my waist so she can rub her pussy against my cock.

"God, Jude..."

I lift my head and shift to the left to give the other nipple the same attention—this time, lightly grazing my teeth over it to gauge her reaction. She bucks hard into me, and a pleasured groan falls from her lips.

"Fuck, yes."

Finley moves like a wave under me, undulating and seeking something more than the teasing I'm doing now. She pulls her hands away from my head to push at the waistband of her skirt, shimmying it as far down her hips as she can with my body pinned between her legs.

Never taking my eyes off her, I release her nipple from between my lips, step back, and reach for the button on my jeans. Her gaze dips to my hands, and she watches me slowly lower the zipper and free my aching cock while she kicks off her skirt, leaving her in only the tiniest scrap of fabric and the bra below her breasts, forcing them up in an erotic offering.

I stroke my length, fighting back the desire to fuck her like a crazed animal. That isn't who Finley is, isn't what she wants. She doesn't want a man who can't control himself. And I don't want to be that man with her.

Instead, I drop to my knees at the side of the bed and drag her to the edge, spreading her legs wide and giving me access to her most sacred spot. She pants wildly as I drag my finger over the black strip covering her already-soaked pussy, and I push it to the side to slip a finger inside her.

Her head falls back on a gasp, and she clenches around me immediately. I grit my teeth and use my free hand to tear away the thong so I can lower my mouth to her cunt.

The first lick is the sweetest thing I've ever tasted in my life. Surrounded by that minty scent she always seems to hold, her flavor coats my tongue and makes my cock weep pre-cum while I stroke it with my other hand.

She whimpers and moves her hips against my face, wanting more, and as much as I would love to have her come down my throat, no matter how badly I want to see her fall apart that way, I'm going to come before the main attraction if I don't stop right now.

I rise to my feet, position myself at her slick opening, and plunge inside the welcoming heat I've been dreaming about and never thought I would ever get to experience.

Fucking hell.

FINLEY

SWEET MOTHER OF GOD...

Jude sinks into me, his thick cock spreading me open, filling me, finally giving me what I wanted for what feels like so long.

Has it really only been two weeks since I met this man? Since he walked into that tiny room in the jail and looked through me with the same blazing blue eyes he has locked on me now?

It can't possibly be, not with the way my heart thunders against my chest, my body craving everything from him and frantically trying to get it. His lips against my skin, tongue dragging through my pussy and gliding over my clit wound me up so tightly, it felt like I might explode, but now that I have him inside me, I can barely breathe.

He tugs his shirt off over his head, exposing his hard, lean body, marred with vicious scars visible even in the darkness of the apartment. I feather my fingers over them, and he stills inside me, buried so deep it feels like he's reached to the very core where I hide all the things I've longed for and didn't think I could find or have without sacrificing everything I worked so hard to obtain.

Blue eyes swimming with lust find mine, and he pulls my hand away from his chest and kisses my fingers lightly as he gradually withdraws. I groan and let my eyes drift closed at the almost agonizingly slow movement. He tugs my hand above my head and does the same with the other, pinning them there as he stares down at me with a barely contained wildness tightening his jaw.

He pulls out and pumps into me again. My hips bow up to meet his, and every time, I clench around him, letting the head of his cock drag along that spot deep inside me, sending ripples of pleasure across my skin and heat surging through my blood.

This is crazy and frantic, a combustion of two volatile forces thrown together in an impossible situation. We were doomed to fail, set on this collision course with each other the moment he set foot in New York. There was nothing we could have done to stop this once our eyes met, once we truly *saw* each other.

There was no turning back.

Fighting it was futile.

We shouldn't have even tried.

I knew what coming here tonight would mean.

After the realization I had about what Jude was doing—why he's here—it all became so crystal clear.

Why things felt different with him from day one. Why I wasn't treating him like other clients. Why he never seemed like a criminal.

Because he doesn't hold that kind of selfish hostility toward the law. He's a good man, torn apart by a brutal injury, who just wants to do something good for the world.

He isn't a monster.

Far from it.

But buried inside me like this, I can see the animal lurking within him, the beast that drives him to act where so many won't. A man seeking justice where there is none and fighting himself at the same time.

Every muscle in his body tenses, each shove inside me coiling him tighter and tighter until it looks like he's going to snap. His grip on my hands loosens, and I wrap my hands around his neck and drag his mouth to mine, kissing him deeply, tasting myself there along with his own unique flavor born of strength, danger, aggression, and pride.

Jude Lawson is a man who has always fought—for his country, for his life, for people he thought needed protecting, and now, he's fighting with himself, holding back for fear of hurting me or maybe himself, keeping himself from letting loose everything he's bottled up inside for so long.

All his anguish.

All his pain.

All the reasons he keeps silent and builds up walls around himself.

Walls I want to disappear.

I want to see them shatter so the man who's hidden behind them can finally be free—at least for tonight.

We can deal with the fallout of this tomorrow.

I suck his lip into my mouth and bite down, and he releases a heavy groan that vibrates through his chest and into my body as he plunges deeper into me. Each stroke, his fingers tighten on my hips, and I capture his face between my hands. His neck strains, sweat beading across his forehead.

"Don't hold back, Jude." I clench around him, trying to enforce my words as much as the friction. "Don't hold *anything* back."

"F-f-fuck." He pulls out sharply and slaps the side of my thigh. "G-g-get on your kn-kn-knees."

His low, gravelly voice, heavy with need, forces me to roll over and up onto my knees, raising my ass into the air and toward him. He grips my hips and drives into me again, going so much deeper, feeling impossibly bigger this way.

"God, yes." My words tumble out on a gasp. "Like that."

A strong hand at the middle of my shoulder blades forces me down, and I lower my chest and face to the mattress, turning my head to the side to watch his raw power and beauty as he fucks me.

The new position makes him grit his teeth, his muscles straining so hard it looks like they'll burst. Every thrust of his hips forces him deeper into my body and soul.

He's not the kind of man you walk away from. Not the kind of man you can forget. Not the kind of man you can resist. Not even if it might cost you what you love more than anything.

Jude grips my side with his left hand while the other grasps my hair and tugs, jerking my head back and up.

Fuck.

It changes the angle slightly. His fingers dig into my flesh, his grip on my hair tightening, too. A few more long, hard strokes are all it takes for the blazing heat to spread and ripple across my skin and out through my limbs. He rolls his hips up with each thrust, giving another sharp tug on my hair until tiny pinpricks of pain flash across my scalp.

My orgasm comes quickly, a cataclysm of pleasure erupting from my core and out to every cell in my body. I gasp and jerk on his cock as he continues to plow into me relentlessly, his entire body shaking violently, seeking his own release.

He lets go of my hair and grips my other hip, tugging me toward him and tilting me up until he's ramming down, driving into me like a drill trying to get to the center of something, or maybe he's trying to cement himself inside me, prove something to both me and to the lingering questions in his mind about how I feel about him, about this.

With my body still twitching, ecstasy still coursing through my veins, he races toward his own orgasm, dragging mine out until I can't catch my breath and fully fall onto the bed.

If he only knew what we were risking, what *I* am.

Maybe that's what makes this so hot—the fact that we can both lose big.

He releases a strangled groan and pushes into me one final time, coming deep inside me before he feathers his lips to my neck and collapses on top of me.

His hard body pins me down, cocooning me in strength, sweat, and hot skin. Warm breath flutters against my ear, heavy and labored. His heart beats rapidly against my shoulder blade, matching the rhythm of my own.

It's one minute of peace.

A chance to linger in the ecstasy of the moment.

To forget the world outside and what it expects of us.

Because all too soon, reality is going to slap us in the face.

In the stark light of morning, we'll see what we've done. We'll have to acknowledge the problems it has caused. We'll see everything we risked for this moment. And we'll have to deal with the consequences.

I let myself sink into the strong arms of the man who is worth so much more than he knows, who has made me reconsider everything, who has made me see who and what he really is, who has let me into his fragile, shattered world even if only for one night.

His calloused fingertips brush along my spine, and I shudder as goosebumps break out across my skin. He skims his lips over my skin, letting them linger there, offering featherlight brushes that ignite that fire in my blood again as his cock hardens, still inside me.

He rolls his hips forward, jamming himself deeper,

and I moan and arch toward him. One strong arm wraps around my waist, molding me to him, as he languidly draws his hips back before driving himself into me again.

Any rational thoughts flee on the wave of renewed ecstasy.

Jude's lips find the nape of my neck and kiss up to my ear. "F-f-fuck you f-f-feel good."

His words, the ones he never shares with anyone else, resound loudly in my head. He's giving me something he never gives anyone else.

This isn't Mouth. He's giving me Jude.

13

FINLEY

I finally push back from my desk, after what has been an absolute killer week full of complications I never could have seen coming, and release a deep groan.

My body still aches in all the best ways after my night with Jude, even while my mind can't stop running over the fact that I violated every moral and ethical code I've ever believed in to get those glorious results.

I can't get out of here fast enough. Spending some time at home, away from the office, away from Jude and what he does to me, will give me some time to seek some clarity.

Almost as if to say, "fuck you," my phone rings, and I wince and glance at the screen.

Enzo.

My stomach tightens right away. He knows I will call

him if I have any news on his case, so if he's calling me, it can't be good. "Hey, Enzo. What's going on?"

"Um, I have something to tell you that you're not going to be happy about."

Fuck.

I rub at the headache suddenly forming at my temples. "What happened?"

"Well...I went to Danica's house—"

"You *what*?"

"I know. I know, but look, Matthews has been on her since before he got discharged, blowing up her phone and threatening her. You saw the press conference. He implied that he was never going to let her go. I don't trust him, so I went to check on her. But when I was leaving, I saw Matthews' Mercedes parked across the street from her place. I turned around and went right back in and told her she had to leave. She can't stay there anymore, Ms. Banks. Not alone. I took her to Big Nose Kate's and put her in the apartment above it so my dad and the guys can keep an eye on her."

Fucking hell.

Now the Satan's Knights are protecting the key witness in the case against their president's son. If that doesn't *scream* interference with a witness, nothing does.

"So, what you're telling me is that you completely ignored the no-contact order issued by the court as part of your conditions of release on bond, and now, you're going to bring into question the credibility of the only witness we have, and whom we need to potentially get your case dumped, by being personally involved with her?"

Enzo releases a little sigh. "I guess it does sound bad when you put it that way."

"You think?"

"I don't have a choice, Ms. Banks. She's in danger. Matthews is dangerous. And now that he knows she's on my side, it's only going to get worse."

Shit.

He isn't wrong about that. Matthews has to have learned about the statements by now since I sent the affidavit to ADA Waters, and her ex is likely willing to do anything to protect his picture-perfect image for the campaign. Danica's statements could ruin everything for him, and he's already proven he's the kind of man willing to put his hands on a woman—even one he was once married to and supposedly loved.

That puts Enzo—and me—between a rock and a hard place.

Danica clearly needs protection from Matthews. I could call the detectives in charge of the case and tell them everything Enzo just revealed to me, ask them to put a car on Danica and watch to ensure Matthews isn't a problem, but then they'll know Enzo was violating his bond, exposing him to further charges.

"So, you're saying you won't stay away from her and just let her deal with Matthews on her own?"

"That's not an option. I won't abandon her."

That's what I thought.

Deep down, despite who his father is and the type of

people he grew up around, he's a good guy and thinks he's doing the right thing.

"I want you to listen very carefully to me, Enzo. Having contact with Danica or Matthews is a violation of the terms of your release. If the district attorney's office finds out, they will issue additional felony charges against you, ones to which we have no defense like we do the original charge. My legal advice as your attorney is to abide by the terms of your bond and have no contact with either of them." I inhale deeply and release a sigh. "If you do, don't get caught, and I can't know about it. Do you understand?"

"Understood."

He better. If this goes sideways because he couldn't stay away from Danica and he ends up going to prison, the Knights will have my—and likely Schwartz's—head for it. It won't matter that his own choices and actions got him into the situation; I'm the one who is supposed to get him out.

The intercom on my desk phone buzzes just as I set down my cell phone, and Terri clears her throat. "Um, ma'am, there's a Mr. Lawson here to see you."

"What?" I jerk my head toward my closed door. "Um, okay, I'll be right out."

Shit. What the hell is he doing here?

I force myself to my feet and walk to the door, but I can't seem to make my hand twist the knob. Not when I know what is waiting for me out there. *Who* is waiting for me.

The man who utterly destroyed all the walls I had

built around my heart, decimated my ethics and values, and made me come more times than I could count last night.

I stand, staring at my hand for a moment, trying to muster up the courage to walk out there and see him after I slipped out without a word this morning. It was a bid to avoid the awkwardness we're about to face right now, and in hindsight, the privacy of his condo seems like a much better place to do this than in my damn office.

Fuckity fuck fuck.

This isn't going to end well, and I need to maintain a professional composure in front of the office staff—and my client.

I pull open the door and walk out to the reception area, holding my breath. Jude stands against one wall, leaning his shoulder to the painted surface, ankles crossed over each other casually—like he isn't here to meet with the woman he just fucked last night.

His blue eyes find mine immediately, and the corner of his lip twitches. But otherwise, he doesn't offer any other reaction or say anything. Not that I would expect him to.

"Mr. Lawson"—I plaster on my most professional smile—"I wasn't expecting to see you today."

He smirks, pushes off the wall, and walks toward me, practically undressing me with his gaze.

I glance at my watch. "I have a few minutes before my next appointment, so we can talk about whatever's on your mind."

Jude pauses next to me and gives me a look that tells me it isn't going to be nearly enough time.

Oh, hell.

I clear my throat and offer a tight smile to Terri. Jude inclines his head toward her in passing and follows me back to my office. Pausing outside the open door, I motion for him to enter first. He strolls past casually, watching me over his shoulder as I step in and close the door behind me, leaning against it and letting out a whoosh of held breath.

"What are you doing here?"

He slowly meanders over to my desk and sits on the edge of it facing me, arms over his barrel chest. "Y-y-you disappeared this morning. T-t-that's usually my j-j-job."

"Ha, ha. Very funny." I step away from the door and take a step toward him. "Is there something wrong?"

A smirk spreads across his lips, and he shakes his head. "C-c-can't I v-v-visit my l-l-lawyer's office?"

I glance down at the monitor on his ankle and the green light flashing there. "Yes. If the meeting has been approved, but I didn't—"

"I c-c-called them this m-m-morning."

He called them and actually spoke to someone on the phone just so he could come down here and see me.

What the hell?

My chest tightens, and sweat breaks out over my skin as he continues to stare at me. "Really, Mouth. What are you doing here?"

MOUTH

Finley shifts nervously on her stilettoed feet, twisting her hands in front of her as she watches me with trepidation that definitely wasn't there twelve hours ago.

This isn't the Finley Banks I know.

She's always so sure of herself. So confident. So unwilling to back down. This version of her is so much more vulnerable—this is the one who spent the night with me, who let me touch her and kiss and take her all night long...and then slipped out while I pretended to still be asleep.

This may be what she's really like underneath all the bravado and armor she wears to do her job in a business that can be misogynistic and volatile. And it didn't slip my notice that she's back to calling me Mouth again, trying to distance herself from the name she called me while I was buried inside her.

I may have let her leave this morning without confronting her or stopping her, giving her the space she clearly needed to mentally sort through what went down between us, but I'm not about to let her pretend last night didn't happen.

It meant too much, even if she wasn't ready to accept that this morning. I've given her the day to think, to figure out how she's going to play this, and I'm done waiting to know how she feels about all this.

"I w-w-wanted to make s-s-sure you w-w-were okay."

Something flashes in her eyes for a second before she closes them and takes a deep breath, flattening her hand against her stomach like she's trying to quiet something fluttering there. "I don't know how to answer that, Mouth. What happened was..."

She trails off like she can't think of the word.

Incredible.

Fantastic.

Mind-blowing.

So many descriptive words come to mind to explain what happened between us, but looking at her, I know the word she's thinking of is *mistake*.

Last night wasn't a mistake, though.

She may be questioning her own actions; given her position, I'd be shocked if she weren't. But us coming together like that was what we both wanted. What we both *needed*. And I won't let her regret it.

Finley averts her gaze, keeping her focus on her feet or the window, anywhere but at me. "Things are very complicated right now, Mouth, and I found myself in a position I thought I would never be in professionally, where I'm having to not only question my ethics but also break the code I vowed when I was sworn in as an attorney in the state of New York." She glances over her shoulder toward the closed door, nervous we might be overheard or interrupted. "I always knew that working with Schwartz would mean I'd have to take cases I wouldn't like and represent people I wouldn't choose to. I accept that because I've always believed that the system only works when everyone is entitled to vigorous representation. But I also believe there are lines which shouldn't be crossed, and lately..." She shakes her head, her eyes shimmering with unshed tears. "Christ, Mouth, I've been crossing all of them."

I stand from the desk and walk over to her, taking her biceps in my hands and rubbing her arms gently. "Y-y-you didn't d-d-do anything wr-wr-wrong."

She releases a sigh. "Yes, I did, Mouth. I did. You're my *client,* and what happened never should have. On top of that, I have knowledge that you are tampering with your surveillance bracelet and willfully violating the bond of the court. And that's the least of your crimes."

You don't know the half of it.

Although, I'm sure she suspects that the bodies that have been turning up have been at my hand, no one will ever prove it, and that's all that matters.

Last night, she said she understood what I was doing, and that didn't make her run because deep down, she knows I'm not in the wrong. That what I'm doing is a form of justice the courts she serves can't give.

This internal war raging through her is going to destroy her.

"It isn't just about you, either. There are other things going on with other clients that just..."

Finley lets out a breath so heavy it actually makes my heart hurt for her. She's a good person who firmly believes that what she's doing is right, and I've helped put her in a situation where her ethics and morals are being smashed to pieces.

That can't continue.

I lift up her chin to force her to meet my gaze. "Y-y-you're f-f-fired."

Her green eyes widen, brows flying up. "What?"

"I-i-if th-th-that's the p-p-problem, t-t-then you're f-f-fired."

"No." She shakes her head, her hands finding the front of my shirt. "You can't. That's not what I—"

I brush my thumb across her lips, silencing her before she can argue with me about this. "I w-w-won't let you f-f-feel guilty about th-th-this."

"You're not firing me. Schwartz is too damn busy to handle your case, and I'm not going to pass this off to anyone else, especially not when I have already spoken with the ADA on the case and have things moving in the right direction." Her gaze locks with mine, determination hardening them, but the affection and fire still blaze in their depths. "What happened just can't happen again."

Just like she knew she should leave but wouldn't last night, I know she doesn't mean it. Not really. She's just still fighting the battle in her own head.

I smirk and lean in until my lips are just short of hers. "B-b-but it's g-g-going to."

No matter what she tries to tell herself, she can't walk away from this any more than I can. If either of us could, we never would have kissed, we never would have fucked each other into mindless bliss last night, and we wouldn't be standing here having this conversation while wanting to be back in my bed.

Finley sighs again and sags slightly, her fingers curling into the soft material over my chest. "I know."

Her green eyes hold mine for a moment, both of us

resigned to the fact that this is happening and there isn't any hope of stopping it.

I press my lips against hers softly, then release her chin and step back from her. "I'll s-s-see you t-t-tonight."

Without waiting for her response, I step around her, open the door, and move out of her office and toward the reception area.

Finley Banks is one of a fucking kind, and as long as she's going to look past all the reasons I'm all kinds of wrong for her, I'm going do everything I can to make her happy.

Life may have stolen my memories, but my broken body still knew what Finley needed last night and gave it to her.

It may be all I ever *can* give her.

14

MOUTH

'm going to fucking kill him.

The text from Parrish said to head to the marina for "boat washing" and to come quickly. I was just *about* to—inside Finley. This better be a fucking life-or-death style emergency, or I will put a bullet between his fucking eyes and throw him in the damn harbor.

Who the fuck does he think he is?

We teamed up *one* damn time with those Satan's Knights fuckers, and now Parrish acts like I'm his fucking lapdog at his beck and call.

We're going to come to an understanding about that tonight.

Whatever the hell is going on can't be more important than burying myself inside Finley. Nothing is.

I slam the car door and jog the block to the marina,

where Parrish waits near the bait and tackle shop, standing next to his bike, toothpick dangling from his lips. He scans his surroundings carefully, vigilant like he's expecting someone he doesn't want to see to show up at any moment.

Hopefully, it isn't the fucking cops.

The last thing I need right now is to get caught out of the apartment—sans monitor—associating with a member of the fucking Knights and doing God only knows what.

He watches me approach him. "Hey, thanks for coming so quickly."

I grab the front of his shirt and shove him back against the building, his toothpick tumbling to the ground. "I am n-n-not your f-f-fucking dog to c-c-call whenever you n-n-need so-so-something d-d-done."

His eyes widen, and he sneers at me. "Ah, so you do fucking speak. What's the problem, motherfucker? Did I interrupt you fucking your girl?"

Motherfucking asshole.

No one knows about what's going on between Finley and me, and no one *can* know. It would ruin everything for her. Him even joking about me *having* a girl is way too close to the truth for comfort.

I press my face close to his. "N-n-never a-a-again."

Before the notoriously insane man can snap back, the crunch of footsteps approaching from behind me makes me spin toward the sound, gun already pulled, but Parrish grabs my arm.

"No. He's with us."

This douchebag is with us?

The guy approaches, his curly dark hair blowing slightly in the breeze, in dark jeans and a black shirt, staring at me with icy-blue eyes.

Parrish steps between us. "Mouth, this is Mayhem. Mayhem, this is Mouth." A low chuckle slips from his lips. "You two will get along great." He smacks Mayhem in the chest. "You never shut the fuck up, and he"—he glances at me—"well, he's fucking quiet."

Christ. Just what I need. Some asshole named Mayhem fucking up whatever it is Parrish needs me to do.

Mayhem scowls at him. "I don't need a babysitter."

"You need whatever the fuck I say you need." Parrish issues a growl. "If you hadn't fucked up the Matthews hit by going after Guthrie instead, we wouldn't even be in this situation."

I dart my gaze between the two men.

This *asshole is the reason I had to threaten Guthrie and couldn't just whack him? They're protecting* this *guy?*

Parrish answers my unspoken question with an exasperated sigh and nods toward Mayhem. "Listen up, fucker. You two have different skills, and this is extremely personal to me. Don't *fuck* this up. It has to look like a suicide."

Oh, hell.

Parrish glances around to ensure we're alone. "It's Brent Matthews. Apparently, he grabbed Enzo's girl, brought her to his boat, and argued with his partner, Guthrie. They fought, and Matthews killed him and threw him into the water. Enzo arrived in time to stop him from taking Danica anywhere else, but he had to use a tire iron to do it. We need it to look like he did this himself so there aren't any questions."

Fucking hell.

I incline my head, indicating I got it. No wonder Parrish wanted me here. This Mayhem guy is clearly a fucking moron who can't do a job properly. Parrish needs to ensure this is done right to protect the son of his president, and I'm the only one he knows can do it who isn't tied to the club.

Just my fucking luck.

But somehow, it almost seems fitting that I be the one to clean up this mess. Considering what I've learned about Guthrie and Matthews over the last couple of weeks, they would have met their end through my scope eventually anyway.

I turn away from Parrish and make my way toward the dock.

Mayhem hustles after me. "Okay, here's what we need to do—"

With a hard tug on his shirt, I swing him around to face me. His eyes meet mine, and I shake my head and point to myself.

He raises a confused brow. "What?"

Motherfucking fuck.

"Bro, we need to hustle here. You know, time is of the essence and shit."

Why the hell did Parrish saddle me with this guy?

This is something I could have handled alone in my sleep, but he had to bring in Chatty Cathy over here. I pull out my notebook and start to write while Mayhem shifts nervously.

"No time to journal, asshole. Let's fucking go!"

I rip out the page and slam it into his chest, knocking him back a few steps, almost into the damn water. He pulls the paper up and reads it.

I'm in charge!

"You needed that in print?" He stares at me for a moment like he's trying to figure something out. "Are you mute?"

Somehow, I stop my fist an inch from connecting with his face.

We don't have time for this bullshit.

I scribble in my notebook again, rip out the page, and hand it to him before making my way onto the boat.

NO! I'll tell you what to do!

"I do this very well. Thank you very fucking much."

Unfuckinglikely.

This guy is clearly a fucking amateur playing at being whatever the fuck it is he thinks he is. If I left him in charge, we'd be cuffed and in a jail cell before the damn sun comes up and the Knights would be fucked, their prez's son in the slammer for murder.

I growl at him and step onto the boat.

Matthews' body lies in the center of the cabin, a bloody gash on his left temple, a tire iron beside the body. I don't waste any time pulling on my gloves and wiping the weapon clean as I walk to the deck and toss it into the water.

Mayhem reaches into his waistband with a gloved hand and pulls out a Glock. "It's clean. Untraceable."

Huh. Maybe this guy isn't as fucking stupid as he looks.

I squat beside the body and lift his right hand to place the weapon and pull the trigger. The shot will blow out the other side of his temple and destroy any evidence of what Enzo did with the tire iron.

"No." Mayhem squats across from me and lifts the stiff's other hand. "He's a leftie." He wraps the fingers of Matthews' left hand around the gun. "I noticed at that press conference that he made a writing gesture with his left hand. See, he wears his watch on his right hand, too. When cleaning a scene, you have to notice those little details."

Fucking prick.

I would have noticed the watch when I went to put the gun in his hand, but I have to say, it's a nice catch. A half-nod is all the acknowledgment he gets for that as I rise to my feet and move out of the way of the spray about to come.

He grins at me. "Ah, see, we had a little bonding moment there, you and me, big guy. Maybe we'll go grab a beer after?"

I glower at him and shake my head.

"Hate to break up this little bromance, but..." Mayhem pulls the trigger with Matthews' fingers, the congressional hopeful's brains blowing out across the cabin.

Job done.

And now, I'm done with Parrish, too.

The only good thing the guy ever did for me was introduce me to Finley, and now, I need to figure out what the fuck I'm going to do about that situation— besides get back home and back inside her as quickly as is humanly possible.

FINLEY

JUDE SLIPS in the apartment door, throws the lock behind him, and kicks off his boots before slowly making his way toward the bathroom.

Where were you?

The question sits on the tip of my tongue as I watch him stripping off his clothes and letting them fall to the wood floor. I want to know what was so important that it made him rush out of here in the middle of sex. I want to know what was more important than *me,* than *us* in that moment, but I won't ask because I also *don't* want to know.

His bare shoulders tense, he steps into the bathroom nude, flicks on the light, and nudges the door halfway shut. He cranks on the shower before he returns to stand in front of the mirror, entranced by something reflecting back at him.

What does he see?

My understanding of amnesia is limited, at best, and even though I've read his medical records, I still don't have a grasp on what it means to him on a day-to-day basis.

Does he even recognize himself?

Lately, it's seemed like I'm staring at a stranger when I look in the mirror, so I can't imagine what it might be like for him. From where I still lie on the bed, in the same place he left me, I can't tell what he's doing, but the tension practically rolls off him, reaching me even over here.

Whatever he was just out doing, it rattled him for some reason. He's come back a different man than he was when he left only a few hours ago.

Steam starts to fill the bathroom and pour out into the main loft area, and Jude finally turns toward the shower and steps inside, sliding the glass door closed behind him.

I don't know Jude well enough to know if this is one of those times I should leave him alone, but something compels me to climb from the bed and pad into the bathroom.

He stands under the spray, his face raised to it, arms stiff at his side, hands fisted. I take a step closer, and he flinches, his head twitching slightly toward me.

There isn't any way to hide that I'm here now. I could turn around and go back to bed alone, wait for him to come out after he's decompressed from whatever happened, but something about that doesn't feel right.

This isn't the time to abandon him to his own head.

I slide the shower door open and step in behind him, wrapping my arms around his waist and resting my face against my back. "You weren't going to tell me you're back?"

He doesn't have a response, at least not one he's going to offer. Likely because he doesn't want to have to answer questions about where he was or what he was doing tonight.

We're on unsteady ground, and he won't risk shaking it by answering any more than I do by asking those questions.

I brush my lips to his spine, squeezing him gently. "Are you okay?"

That seems like a safe question to ask, one that leaves him plenty of room to give whatever answer he wants.

Jude glances over his shoulder at me, the water still pounding his chest, and watches me for a moment before he nods.

I swim in his blue eyes, searching for the lie in the statement he didn't even make. "I'm not going to ask you what you were doing if that's what you're worried about."

He clenches his jaw and turns to face me.

I stare up at him, pressing my hands against his chest. "I won't ask. I don't want to know. I'll never ask if you don't want to tell me."

Our nakedness and proximity, or maybe my words, make his cock harden between us, and he grasps my hips and crushes me against him, crushing his lips to mine like I'm the only one who can provide the oxygen he needs to breathe in this moment.

Sometimes it feels like that for me, too, like everything that's going on in my head, all the cases, all the lives in my hands, are all so overwhelming that I can't focus on anything because I don't have the air to make my body work properly.

I score my nails down his chest, over his abs, and circle his cock. My first stroke drags a low groan from his lips against mine, and I work him tenderly, slowly, trying to show him that life doesn't always have to be so painful or fast.

His body tenses more, and I pull away from his kiss.

Wide blue eyes meet mine and watch me lower myself to my knees under the hot spray.

Jude has made me feel so good and done this for me so many times that I can't think of a better way to help him find his release from whatever is weighing so heavily on him.

I take his cock in my mouth and drag my tongue along the bottom of it.

"F-f-fuck, Finley."

His hands tangle in my wet hair as water beats against his back, sluicing over his shoulders and down over me. I let his cock pop free of my lips and grip at the base so I can lift it up to lick and suck all along the shaft, swirling my tongue around the head.

"Christ, is th-th-there anything you aren't g-g-good at?"

I grin against his flesh at the compliment and with

the knowledge that this is driving him as insane as it is me. Suctioning my mouth around him fully, I reach down with my right hand and swirl my finger around my throbbing clit, needing the friction to dispel the pressure building there the longer I do this to Jude.

Watching him come undone, seeing him forget whatever was plaguing him while I suck his cock is the greatest feeling in the world, and I only want to do more.

I swallow him even deeper, so far down my throat that the head of his cock hits the soft fleshy part at the back that might make anyone else gag, but I just continue to swallow, desperate to taste him on my tongue.

His fingers tighten in my hair, and he shoves his hips forward, coming straight down my throat in hot bursts. I rub at my clit feverishly, wanting to get there with him, to feel the same release, but he jerks me from his length and glances down, eyes zeroing in on where my hand moves between my legs.

He reaches down and jerks me to my feet, molding his mouth to mine in a soul-searing kiss, his own cum still lingering on my tongue. It doesn't seem to bother him, though, his dick growing even harder where it presses against my stomach. He lifts me, turning us to slam me against the cool tile wall, and drives into me in one swift motion.

I gasp and drop my head back against the tile, my moan echoing off it and around in the bathroom as he pumps into me, driving me harder against the wall with each aggressive thrust.

It's like he doesn't know any other way to be with me. Each time is this frantic rush, as if he can't get inside me or make me come fast enough, like he's trying to meld us together permanently before the entire world might collapse around him.

And I love it.

My body craves it. Yearns for it. Reaches for it, for *him* every time he's near.

He pummels me, his strokes harsh and aggressive.

Exactly what he and I need.

"God, Jude. Fuck me harder. Harder."

I dig my nails into his shoulders, digging my feet into his lower back for leverage as he demolishes me, taking out his anger at life or whatever else it might be tonight through me. Then he suddenly stills, and I open my eyes to meet his concerned ones.

"I'm s-s-sorry."

"For what?"

Tears pool in his eyes as he struggles to find the answer. The pain is too much for me to bear, and I grip the back of his head and drag it to me to kiss away his agony.

I press my forehead to his, and he keeps pumping into me, slowing his pace, changing from frantic to long, languid strokes.

It's torture.

A form I can't survive.

I shake my head from side to side. "No, harder. I need it. I need you like this."

His brow furrows like he can't comprehend why I

would want him like that—uncontrolled, wild, reckless. He doesn't see it, doesn't understand why it's what we both need. That we've both been waiting for someone who can give us that.

He renews his harder, faster strokes, and another orgasm starts to tingle at my core. Jude grinds his pelvis on my clit, giving me as much friction as he can while the water pours down over us. His mouth finds mine again, and we kiss and pant against each other's lips until my body stiffens, my pussy tightening and clasping at his cock to drag out his orgasm.

It doesn't take long before we're both finding that release.

Jude groans and collapses against me on the wall, still embedded deep inside me.

I skim my lips against his neck softly, kissing my way up to his ear. "Don't ever apologize for that, Jude. Never."

15

MOUTH

Neither the fresh air nor the nicotine flowing in my veins can stop the overwhelming anxiety coursing through me, making my foot bounce up and down on the metal grate of the fire escape.

I take another drag and hold the smoke in my lungs for a few seconds before I blow it out, watching it curl up to the steps and dissipate into the soft light of early morning.

The hours I've sat out here thinking haven't helped clarify any of the questions endlessly floating through my head since I returned last night. Lying next to Finley while she slept so peacefully only made it worse. Which is why I'm a quarter of a pack in and still don't feel any better about the situation I've created.

Less than twelve hours ago, I helped cover up a murder, and I didn't even feel bad about it. But as soon as

I walked in and saw Finley in my bed, guilt ate away at my stomach, wondering what she would think about what I had done.

And then I took out my frustration on her in a way I never should have, even if she asked for it.

Don't ever apologize for that, Jude. Never.

Her words ring in my ears even now, but it's impossible not to contemplate how different our worlds are, how different *we* are, and how, in the end, that is what is going to pull us apart.

I sense her before I hear or see her—my skin heating under her careful assessment from inside the apartment. Finley climbs out the window and onto the fire escape in one of my T-shirts that hangs down to her mid-thigh.

She offers me a little half-smile as I take another drag. "I didn't know you smoke."

"S-s-sometimes." I drop it to my feet and grind it out with my boot. "I sh-sh-shouldn't."

Finley rests her arms against the metal railing in front of her and looks out across the city. "There's a lot I don't know about you. I don't even know what happened to you to cause your injuries." She glances over at me with pain in her eyes that makes my chest tighten. "I don't even know what your favorite food is."

It's the same realization that has occupied my thoughts the last few hours—how little we actually know about each other and the fact that I don't even know most of it about myself unless someone else tells me.

At least one of those is easy to answer.

I reach out and wrap my arm around her thighs,

dragging her toward me to stand between my legs and press my face against her lower belly. "Y-y-you know exactly wh-wh-what my favorite thing to e-e-eat is."

A tiny laugh shakes her body, but when I pull back my head and look up at her, the pink blush on her cheeks doesn't hide the pain still etched on her face. "I barely know you. It's only been two fucking weeks, and I'm in bed with my client." She runs her hands through my hair lazily. "What are we doing, Jude? What am *I* doing?"

It's a fair question.

Finley's been an open book for me about her reservations and her life, chattering on about growing up in a small town in Illinois before coming to New York for undergrad and then ultimately law school at Fordham, where she met David Schwartz, who she now works with. She's never afraid to just keep talking, to hold a one-sided conversation when she knows I can't or won't respond or interject.

Someone else might be annoyed by it, but her voice has become my favorite sound—especially when she's moaning my name while I'm inside her.

She's told me so much about herself, revealed everything, but I can't say the same. And it isn't just because all I remember are bits and pieces and the only things I really *know* are what's been told to me.

I don't *want* her to know me when I don't even know myself. I want to protect her from what I'm capable of, what I plan on continuing to do. The things she's come so close to being on the wrong side of since she met me.

She continues to thread her fingers through my hair, correctly assuming I don't want to answer her. "The only things I know about you are what I read in your medical records and the information Reaper gave me so I could get you out on bond."

I'd love to keep it that way.

The less she knows, the easier it will be to walk away when she realizes I'm completely wrong for her, that I have nothing to offer her except mind-bending sex, when she sees how *truly* broken I am—beyond what was written on those pages in my medical records.

She retreats a step from me, her distress at my reluctance to open up to her, making her not even want my touch. Her green eyes plead with me, though they hold no anger, just affection and confusion that I'm sure mine match.

Finley deserves an answer.

She deserves everything.

It's the least I can give her.

"I o-o-only remember b-b-bits and pieces. The r-r-rest, my fr-fr-friends t-t-old me. M-m-my parents b-b-both died over a d-d-decade ago—my d-d-dad from cancer and my m-m-mom a heart attack. I'm n-n-not in contact with my s-s-sisters anymore. M-m-mostly because I d-d-didn't know them when I w-w-woke up and w-w-wouldn't l-l-let them h-h-help me."

She waits patiently for me to continue, and I swallow through my dry throat. This might be the most I've spoken in almost five years—the most I've wanted to, but the subject matter is more painful than just about anything else.

"I h-h-have these little fl-fl-flashes of m-m-memories from growing up. G-g-going ice sk-sk-skating. Christmas t-t-trees and pr-pr-presents under them. But I ca-ca-can't piece them t-t-together into any o-o-one solid m-m-memory. It's all j-j-just jumbled. The only th-th-thing I don't seem to st-st-struggle with is d-d-doing th-th-this."

I spread my hands wide, knowing she will understand exactly what I'm talking about without saying the words.

"For s-s-some r-r-reason, even though my m-m-memories are sh-sh-shattered, my instincts are all st-st-still there. E-e-everything I was tr-tr-trained to d-d-do. If y-y-you hand me a r-r-rifle, I'll have it dis-dis-disassembled in under th-th-thirty seconds without e-e-even th-th-thinking about it. But a-a-ask me my b-b-birthday and I w-w-wouldn't know it unless s-s-someone else t-t-told me."

A single tear trickles down Finley's cheek, and she quickly swipes it away.

I let out a deep sigh and scrub my hand over the stubble on my face. "I s-s-sometimes remember h-h-hunting with my d-d-dad when he w-w-wasn't deployed. T-t-turns out, I w-w-was very g-g-good at it."

Despite the heavy topic, a smile tilts her lips. "Somehow, that doesn't surprise me."

"I enlisted o-o-out of h-h-high school, and my p-p-particular skill w-w-was picked up on v-v-very early in my c-c-career. I w-w-was in t-t-the R-r-rangers first as a sn-sn-sniper, then m-m-moved to D-d-delta Force.

She nods slowly. "That sure explains a lot. I requested your military records, but I kept hitting a wall with getting them."

"I m-m-managed to make it th-th-through m-m-most of my c-c-career relatively unscathed u-u-until that f-f-final deployment wh-wh-when an RPG h-h-hit the b-b-building I w-w-was in."

Her brow furrows. "So, that's how it happened?"

I nod slowly, bits and pieces of the memory flashing in my head.

Scanning the village square.

Shots coming from another building.

Reaper's voice in my ear.

The world exploding around me.

Pain.

"I d-d-don't remember it. At l-l-least, not all of it. R-r-reaper p-p-pulled me from the ru-ru-rubble and got me o-o-out of there. I'd be d-d-dead if it w-w-weren't for him."

And so many days since then, I wished he would have just left me there. It would have been easier to go out that way than to live like this.

"And the headaches?"

I wince and rub at the back of my neck. "Th-th-they get especially b-b-bad when I'm st-st-stressed, b-b-but sometimes they c-c-come for no r-r-reason at all." I pause for a moment and look at her, considering not revealing the thing that's been on my mind since we first met. "E-e-ever s-s-since I m-m-met you, I've di-di-discovered something."

One of her eyebrows wings up. "What's that?"

"Wh-wh-when we're t-t-together, wh-wh-when you're w-w-with me, they s-s-seem to g-g-go away."

She considers me for a moment, then offers a humorless laugh, shaking her head. "That isn't me doing that, Jude; it's just my perfume."

"Wh-wh-what?"

A sad smile turns her lips. "It's my perfume. The main ingredients are citrus and peppermint, which have been used for hundreds of years to treat headaches. Feeling good around me has nothing to do with *me* and everything to do with *that*."

I reach out and grab her again, dragging her to me. "N-n-no, it d-d-doesn't. That m-m-may b-b-be a side effect. But it's y-y-you. I haven't f-f-felt alive. I haven't f-f-felt like I was w-w-worth anything f-f-for so l-l-long th-th-that I f-f-forgot what it f-f-felt l-l-like to w-w-want something and be w-w-wanted by someone."

She stares down at me with tears pooling in her eyes.

"Y-y-you g-g-gave me all th-th-that, and I d-d-don't kn-kn-know wh-wh-what to d-d-do with it. All I kn-kn-know is that I d-d-don't w-w-want to lose it. I d-d-don't want to l-l-lose y-y-you. But it already f-f-feels l-l-like I'm going to."

FINLEY

I STARE DOWN at the man I should have walked away from the moment I saw him because I knew there was something there. Something different. Something I hadn't felt before.

An attraction.

A desire.

A need and a pull toward something that was dangerous and wild yet controlled in a way I couldn't possibly fathom.

And the more I got to know Jude, the more he let me in, the easier it was to fall for him and the harder it becomes to walk away. Yet, the reality of who we are and where we're heading isn't something we can ignore anymore.

"You're going back to Baltimore. As soon as your case is resolved, you'll return to work with Reaper and your other friends. You're going to go do"—I wave a hand absently, not really ready to voice what it is he does —"whatever it is you do in other places, and I'm going to be here defending other criminals."

A smile twitches at the corners of his mouth. "Th-th-that's h-h-how you s-s-see me?"

His question holds no malice, and he doesn't seem offended—more hurt. Which is almost worse.

I shake my head and release a sigh. "I don't know what to think. The day I met you, I knew you were different than my other clients. I saw something, felt something, that told me whatever was going on, what-ever the situation was that put you in that jail, was not what it appeared. And I was right."

When I look at him, I don't see a criminal. I don't see a bad man doing bad things. I see a good man doing what he believes is right. But those are often two sides of the same coin—one that has a very heavy weight.

"I don't think you're a criminal, but I don't know if I can just pretend it doesn't bother me to know what you're out doing at night."

He flinches but doesn't interrupt me.

"Yes, I represent criminals and defend them in court, but what you're doing is different, something that dances the line between good and bad. I believe in the justice system, believe everyone has the right to a defense and the protection of the law. If one of my clients has a case dismissed because the state did an illegal search or there wasn't enough evidence, am I going to find him dead in a few weeks, a bullet through his head or chest because you and your friends deemed it justice?"

I raise an eyebrow at him in question, but when he opens his mouth to answer, I shake my head. "I don't want to know. That was a rhetorical question. I just don't know how to navigate this, Jude. Don't know how to justify it in my head."

If that's even possible.

For the first time I can remember, I truly am at a loss for words. The more I say, the larger the rock in my throat becomes, the more I'm convincing myself that this has to end now before things get even more complicated between us, before I let things go any further.

Jude pushes to his feet and takes my face between his palms. "I kn-kn-know this is h-h-h-ard for y-y-you. Y-y-you may not agree w-w-with everything I d-d-do, but y-y-you kn-kn-know I would n-n-never h-h-hurt you, r-r-right?"

The pain in his eyes as he asks the question makes another tear trickle from my eye. "Jesus, Jude, of course, I know that. I know you could never hurt me. You would never hurt me." I shake my head, trying to collate my disjointed thoughts into something that makes sense. "I understand why you do what you do. Sometimes people slip through the cracks or walk away from crimes when they shouldn't. I've represented people I wish I hadn't, seen people walk out of court free, who I know will re-offend immediately, but it doesn't mean I agree with you and your friends being judge, jury, and executioner, and I don't know if I can ever be okay with it."

"I u-u-understand."

"No." Another tear drops down my face. "You don't, because I should walk away right now, get your case resolved, and then watch you leave."

"B-b-but you w-w-won't?"

He watches me, waits for me to answer the ultimate question.

Can I just turn my back on Jude and whatever this is?

I wrap my arms around his neck and press my forehead against his. "I don't think I can, even if I tried. I've never felt like this before. Never needed or wanted anything as much as I do this. And that's absolutely terrifying for me."

Jude pulls back slightly. "Wh-wh-when I w-w-woke up

in that h-h-hospital and r-r-realized I didn't kn-kn-know who I w-w-was, w-w-when the d-d-doctors t-t-told me my d-d-diagnosis, I th-th-thought my life w-w-was o-o-over, but n-n-now"—he brushes his lips over mine—"I s-s-see it d-d-differently. I've been g-g-given a c-c-clean slate. A ch-ch-chance to st-st-start over, but I'll n-n-never be n-n-normal, Finley. My b-b-brain will n-n-never work r-r-right. My w-w-words will n-n-never come out r-r-right."

The fact that he feels the need to apologize for that, to explain what a future with him would be like, makes my heart ache for him. "I just can't have you going silent on me, Jude."

"I c-c-can't guarantee th-th-that won't ha-ha-happen at t-t-times. I've sp-sp-spent f-f-four years being s-s-silent, wr-wr-writing my words rather than sp-sp-speaking them so n-n-no one kn-kn-knows how truly f-f-fucked up I am. I d-d-don't kn-kn-know how to retrain m-m-myself to get used to t-t-talking again."

I smile at him. "You're doing just fine."

He barks out a laugh that releases a tiny bit of the tension from the moment. "I'm n-n-not, but th-th-thank you."

Tangling my fingers in his hair, I feather my lips over his. "I'll help you figure it out. We'll figure it out—together. Your clean slate may be chipped and broken, but it's not an end. It's a new beginning, one that we have together."

He raises an eyebrow at me. "You're s-s-sure?"

"I'm sure. Now all I have to do is get your case

dismissed so I don't lose my license because I fell in love with my client."

His body stiffens, and his eyes narrow slightly. "R-r-really?"

I hadn't even thought those words until they came out of my mouth. It's crazy. Impossible. People don't fall in love in two weeks. But the words feel right. *Saying* it does.

"Yes, really. I don't know how it happened, but I fell in love with you, Jude. Every fucked-up, broken piece of you."

He grins at me, tightening his hold. "Finley, I l-l-love you, too."

No one else has ever said that to me—at least, not someone I wasn't related to. Most people wouldn't believe it possible, wouldn't accept the words as true in this situation, but with Jude, I know every single thing he says is the absolute truth, or he wouldn't bother to speak it.

"We'll figure this out, Jude."

"A cl-cl-clean slate."

"A clean slate."

16

FINLEY

The phone on my desk buzzes. "I have ADA Waters calling for you."

I stare at it for a moment before I pick it up. If he's calling, it's either to talk about Enzo's case or Jude's. While I'd love to have both wrapped up quickly, resolving Jude's case would mean he's free to go back to Baltimore, and I'm not ready to think about what that will mean for the future we hope to have together.

My hand shakes, picking up the receiver. "This is Attorney Banks."

"Hi, Finley. It's Jon Waters." He gives a humorless laugh. "And apparently, today is your lucky day."

"Why's that?"

"Did you see the news this morning?"

What?

"No."

I was too busy talking to Jude out on the fire escape and then going back in to let him devour me again. It's a wonder I even made it into the office at all today. If Jude had his way, I would still be wrapped up with him in bed.

"Well, Brent Matthews blew his brains out last night."

"*What*?"

"Yeah, on his boat. After apparently killing his business partner, Guthrie, and dumping him into the harbor. The bodies were discovered this morning."

"Holy shit."

He releases an annoyed sigh. "Which means...we no longer have a victim in Enzo Scotto's case and will be moving to dismiss it."

Oh, my God.

Jude got a text message and disappeared last night, and when he came back, he was tense, upset about something. Not himself at all.

Did he have anything to do with this?

I shake my head to dispel the question because I don't *want* to know the answer. Whatever happened, it resolved Enzo's case, and I need to concentrate on my client. "Well, that's good news for Mr. Scotto, then."

"It certainly is, and I would say awfully convenient, too, but he clearly had nothing to do with whatever went down between those two."

"I'm sure he will be happy to know he's no longer facing charges."

"Oh, I'm sure he will. Now, as far as Mr. Lawson is concerned, I have reviewed his medical records."

"Very interesting read, aren't they?"

More like depressing, painful, traumatizing.

He releases a heavy sigh—one that carries the weight of the job he has to do on a daily basis. "I have to tell you, Ms. Banks. It does me no pleasure prosecuting somebody with a history like this, but if I just dismiss these charges, everybody and their brother is going to think it's okay to run around killing people they believe deserve it."

"No, they won't, Jon, and you and I both know that. Mr. Lawson isn't a threat to the community."

Just my heart.

I glance at my copy of the records still stacked on the corner of my desk. "If he did this, and that's a big *if*, he's doing the community a *service*. Doing *you* a service and the *police* a service by taking these guys off the streets. It might be strictly outside the letter of the law. I can concede that. But it doesn't mean it's wrong."

ADA Waters probably isn't the person to be getting into this ethical debate with, especially when I myself have issues with Jude's nighttime activities, but sometimes, it takes being frank with the opposing side to get things done.

"What do you expect me to tell my boss, Ms. Banks?"

"The truth—that you can't prove your case."

He grumbles something under his breath about vigilantes and bloodsucking defense attorneys. "Okay, fine. I'll dismiss *without* prejudice, but if he steps out of line, or if the gun ever turns up and his fingerprints are on it, then I'm going to reissue the charges."

"That's not going to happen."

I never asked Jude what he did with the gun that night, but he's smart enough to have put it somewhere it will never be found, before he got arrested.

"Then, I guess it really *is* your lucky day, Ms. Banks. Double lucky."

"It appears it is."

Though, luck had nothing to do with it. I'm certain the Matthews situation resolving was more than what it appeared, and getting Jude's case resolved is more to do with who *he* is than luck.

"I'll see you next week at the status conferences on these cases, and we'll dismiss them then."

I end the call with a grin spread across my face until I glance up and see Schwartz leaning against my door-frame, looking more haggard and tired than I've ever seen him. "What's wrong?"

He inclines his head toward my phone. "You go first. You look pretty happy about something."

I shove my hands back through my hair, my stomach suddenly turning at the reality of what the news means. "Yeah, I guess you could say that. You can tell Parrish that both Enzo's and Jude Lawson's cases will be dismissed."

Schwartz's eyes widen slightly. "Really?"

I nod. "Apparently, Matthews killed his business partner and then himself last night."

His mouth opens and closes a few times before he finds his words. "Holy fuck."

"Exactly my thoughts."

"So that means Mayhem is likely in the clear, too, since there isn't a victim anymore."

I'm not going to let him in on my suspicions about what Mouth might have done last night because, ultimately, it's irrelevant, and I don't want to know the truth.

"Well, that's exactly what we wanted. All the cases Parrish saddled us with are resolved. Nice fucking work, Fin."

Reclining in my chair, I raise a brow at him. "Thanks. So, why don't you tell me why you look like someone pissed in your Cheerios?"

He rubs the back of his neck as he wanders in, shuts the door, and then makes his way to a chair facing me. "We need to have a talk."

"About what?"

"About something really fucking stupid I did that might change things around here for a while."

Shit.

Schwartz does a lot of stupid stuff, so that statement doesn't narrow it down.

"What happened?"

"Well, that night that you went to Brighton Beach to help Enzo and Mr. Lawson, and I went to Staten Island because I had to deal with the attempted murder."

"Right..."

"I got a flat tire and had to have an Uber bring me there."

"Okay. I'm not following where any of this is going."

"Well, I wound up knowing the Uber driver. She and I were close back in college." He pauses, biting the inside of his cheek. "Until we weren't, and she disappeared. But that's not the point. The point is, I slept with her."

"I'm still not seeing a problem. You sleep with a lot of women, Schwartz."

He smirks. "I do. But she's different, Finley. I knew it back then, but I was too much of a self-absorbed prick to act on it." I stop to point a finger at her. "Before you say anything, I know I'm still self-absorbed, but I'm working on it."

"Holy shit. Are you in love?"

He scowls at me. "Don't talk crazy. No one said anything about love, and it's a delicate situation. It's not just her; she comes with two little girls."

I let my jaw fall open at that revelation. Schwartz isn't exactly kid friendly.

"Don't look at me like that. I think the little one might actually like me." A faint smile wisps across his lips. "She decorated my Ferragamo loafers with stickers, and you *know* how I feel about those shoes."

"They're your babies."

He nods. "And I didn't even flinch. The problem is..." A moment passes where he considers what he's about to tell me. "She's the sister of the victim in one of my cases."

"You're shitting me."

His lips press together in a thin line, and he shakes his head. "I wish I were."

"Did you know?"

"Not when I took the case, but I also didn't have much time to go over the file before the status hearing. She was in the courtroom. I should've walked away, but I didn't. Instead, I took any opportunity to insert myself into her life that I could. And this morning, I told Judge Otto that I've been seeing her."

"Fuck, is he reporting it to the bar?"

"He has to, so there's a good chance I'm going to be looking at a suspension soon."

"Shit." I rub my hands over my face, push back from my desk, and wander over to the window to look out of it rather than at Schwartz while I confess my own indiscretion. "Well, there's something I should tell you, too."

"That doesn't sound good."

I glance over at him and sigh. "It isn't. Or, it wasn't. It might be okay now, I guess."

"What are you talking about?"

Tapping my foot, I cross my arms over my chest, like that might actually do something to protect me from the blowback I'm about to receive. "That call about Mr. Lawson's case getting dropped came at a very good time because I've been sleeping with him."

"You *what*?"

I drop my face in my hands and groan. "I know."

"You are sleeping with a client..."

"Christ, I know how bad that sounds, how bad it is, but Schwartz"—I finally force myself to turn around and look at him again—"you don't understand this man. I tried to keep things professional, tried to act only as his lawyer, but whenever I got near him, everything I was supposed to be doing slipped away, like I wasn't even in control of my own mind or body anymore."

"You could lose your license *permanently* for this, Finley. And I thought what *I* did was bad."

I offer him a humorless grin. "Yeah, I have to say, I'm glad you came in here and told me about your indiscretion. It makes me feel a lot better about my own and made telling you easier."

"Fuck." He drops his elbows to his knees and scrubs his hands over his face. "We really fucked up big time, didn't we?"

"Yep." I walk over to him and lower myself into the chair next to him. "But I think it will be okay. Waters is dismissing Jude's case at the status next week, and it's not like we had planned to go public with our relationship anyway. If anyone *does* find out, it would be after my representation of him is complete, and it wouldn't be an ethical violation anymore. No one but you knows anything happened before that point."

He lifts his head, his blue eyes meeting mine. "And you're okay with that? With having violated your ethics?"

I sigh and lean back. "Fuck if I know, Schwartz. Aren't we always doing that in some way in order to do this job?"

Nodding slowly, he sits up straight. "I guess so. I had to come clean with the judge in order to withdraw from the case, but I don't know what I would have done if I were in your situation."

"You think they'll suspend you?"

"Probably. You're going to have to pick up the slack on cases for however long I'm not allowed to practice."

I nod and smile at him. "I'll hold down the fort."

"I know you can."

"I have to ask...is she worth it?"

He doesn't hesitate before answering. "Fuck, yes. Is he?"

"Absofuckinglutely."

MOUTH

IT'S OVER.

I hit send on the text, and even though it's the middle of the night, almost immediately, Reaper starts his reply.

Shit.

The entire reason I waited to tell him was that I wasn't ready to have a conversation about it; I wasn't ready to admit what it meant for me and the woman asleep beside me.

Reaper: Does that mean you're coming home?

I groan and scrub my hand over my face, looking over at Finley sleeping so peacefully. She isn't tormented by her dreams, doesn't dread closing her eyes at night, afraid of what might come. I envy that but watching her sleep somehow makes the fact that I can't easier to accept.

Even if I *could* sleep under normal circumstances, I wouldn't be able to tonight. When she told me what should have been good news about the charges being dropped, it felt like the floor was falling out from under me rather than something to celebrate.

This stupid anklet will be gone in a few days when we finally go to court and get the charges dismissed. It means the end of my confinement and potentially going to prison, but it also means it's the end of this.

I ghost my fingers down Finley's exposed spine, and she shifts in her sleep, rolling toward me and wrapping her arm over my chest, letting her face rest above my heart.

She releases a little contented sigh, totally oblivious to the turmoil twisting me up inside. I run my fingers through her hair, the silky texture so different from the calluses on my fingers.

We couldn't be more different—her in her suits, arguing cases in front of a judge and jury, me using my hands and anything else at my disposal to destroy people. And we've been living in our own isolated world this entire time, wrapped up in each other and what we have together.

Going home.

It's what Finley has been fighting for, to allow me to go *home*. It's what I had planned to do after I took out Yankovich and his cronies, head back to Baltimore, back to the life I was living with the guys, doing these jobs. Go home. But now, the word doesn't seem so simple anymore.

I had one once, a home, with a mother and a father and sisters. A place full of laughter and affection. I felt safe, secure, loved. The memories may not all be there, but the *feelings* are. So, I know what it is; I know it can exist. And I know I haven't felt like that since the moment I woke up in that hospital.

Until now.

The woman in my arms feels more like a home than anywhere else has in the last four years, and the thought of walking away from that, away from her, to return to the kind of life I had back in Baltimore, makes my eyes burn.

We said we would figure it out, that this was a clean slate to start our lives together, but the very real fact is, the only things I know are there, and she is here—in the city that has caused me nothing but grief.

I squeeze her gently and type up a reply to Reaper.

Not for a bit. Will go to court in a week or so to have the charges formally dismissed. Then Parrish wants to have a little celebratory party.

Not that I particularly want to see him or any of the Knights again, but it gives me an excuse to stay longer, to ensure I get more time with Finley before life puts hundreds of miles between us and what we have.

I hit send, knowing I haven't answered the ultimate question.

Where is home?

Reaper, Viktoria, Chaos, and Avery all flicker through my head. All the good times we've had together. The way we've all worked together to make it through seemingly impossible situations.

I can't walk away from them any more than I can the woman sleeping across my chest.

Finley stirs and finally pushes up on her elbow, blinking tired eyes at me in the dark. "Hey, you okay?"

I nod because even if I tried to speak, I'm not sure what words would come out.

She glances at the phone in my hand. "Who are you talking to?"

"R-r-reaper."

Her smile falters a little. "What does he want?"

"T-t-to kn-kn-know when I'm c-c-coming back."

She presses her hand over my heart, resting it there where the heat of her skin can sizzle against mine. "What did you tell him?"

I turn the phone so she can read the text messages, and any humor she had completely disappears with her frown.

"I guess we haven't really talked about that. Because I have been avoiding bringing it up. And I know better than to assume you will."

Despite how unsettled everything feels, I grin at her acknowledgment that she knows me so well and that she's willing to accept all the intricacies my fucked-up self comes with.

I set my phone on the nightstand and drag her up across my body, her breasts pressing to my chest. My cock reawakens between us, but I ignore the desire to drive into her again and instead address the elephant in the room we've both been dancing around. "I d-d-don't want to l-l-leave, but—"

Her green gaze softens. "But it's all you know how to do."

A tiny bit of relief floods through me. She really does understand without me having to explain it.

What I do with Chaos and Reaper *is* all I know. It's the only thing that has felt real, like I'm making a difference and am still useful even though so many parts of me feel useless at times.

"I can't ask you not to go back, Jude. Can't ask you not to keep doing what you're doing with your friends. I won't, but there's a good chance I have to stay here. If Schwartz gets suspended, someone's going to have to handle all the clients until he gets reinstated. And I can't just up and leave him in the lurch like that. Plus, I'd have to take the bar exam in Maryland and—"

I press my finger over her lips to silence her. "I kn-kn-know, and I wouldn't a-a-ask you to give up th-th-this, either."

Her career is her life as much as what I do is mine. She belongs in the courtroom, and taking her out of it would be selfish.

"So?" She presses her lips to my chest. "What do we do?"

"Wh-wh-whatever w-e-we have to."

She chews on the inside of her cheek, considering the logistics of a relationship where we're in two different cities. "One of us traveling back and forth every weekend?"

I shrug. "If th-th-that's what it t-t-takes."

My answer doesn't seem to appease her, though, her

lips twisting down. "And how long before that becomes too much? Before it gets too complicated?"

Complicated.

Now that's a word I'm familiar with. My life has been nothing *but* complications, but I could never, would never think of Finley as one.

I take her face between my hands and kiss her deeply, letting my lips say what my words never can. "N-n-never. Whatever it t-t-takes."

She tilts her head, leaning into my hand. "You really mean that?"

For years, I've withheld my words, relied on other people to know what I am trying to say without having to voice it, but with Finley, I don't want there to be any question about my intent.

"I n-n-never thought I had a ch-ch-chance at a life, at a fu-fu-future, at anything more th-th-than being a machine w-w-working on reflex and tr-tr-training."

Tears fall down her cheeks, and I wipe them away with my thumbs, hating to see her so distressed. "You're so much more than that, Jude."

"I kn-kn-know. Because of y-y-you. N-n-nothing and no one w-w-will get in the w-w-way of that. I pr-pr-promise."

17

TWO WEEKS LATER

MOUTH

Big Nose Kate's is every bit the dive I thought it would be based on the description Reaper gave me after he was here. Being inside it for the little impromptu celebration organized by Parrish, sticking to the floor each time I try to lift my feet, I can't help but love the place—even if the men who operate out of here have complicated my life more than I can even fathom.

It's exactly the kind of bar I would hang out at if I had to choose one, and it fits the Knights perfectly. Skeezy, a little bit dirty, but also homey and welcoming, in a weird sort of way that makes you want to saddle up to the bar and order a cheap beer.

Various members sit at the long-worn piece of wood to my right, and I watch them all carefully, enjoying the dynamics of the group. They remind me so much of how

Chaos, Reaper, and I are when we're together, and a knot forms in my stomach at not being able to remember all the years before my injury—my time with them and all the other men who were part of our unit who didn't make it back.

Finley's soft hand squeezes at the nape of my neck, bringing me back to the present.

Clean slate.

A fresh start.

I keep thinking about our conversation, about how I need to look at this differently than I have been. I got a raw deal. I'm damaged goods that can never be fixed, but if I weren't, none of this would have ever happened.

Reaper may not have sent me on this mission. I might not have ever met Finley. I might not have ever been given a chance to find what Reaper and Chaos have, with a woman who owns my heart, and even though it took getting arrested to get me to this moment, I can't say I would change anything.

Finley leans over from her seat next to me. "Are you okay? You look like you disappeared there for a second."

I nod at her and press a kiss to her cheek, brushing my lips over to her ear. "I'm f-f-fine."

Schwartz eyes us from across the table. The man who is technically Finley's boss still appears a little perturbed at discovering she is now shacking up with one of her former clients, but she keeps reminding him that "former" is the key word here—and what he did wasn't much better.

No one will ever be able to prove when Finley and I

got personally involved. For that reason, "case dismissed" were the sweetest words I've ever heard—next to Finley telling me she loves me—because it meant we were free. Free from the confines of the attorney-client relationship. From everything else that held either of us back. Free to be together and not risk everything she worked so hard for her entire life.

The guilt still lingers over her actions, and she may always struggle with what the guys and I do, but for some reason, I'm not worried anymore. Because I see the way she looks at me, feel the way she clings to me when I'm inside her, hear it in her words when she begs for more and tells me she loves me.

We'll work it out.

We'll overcome any obstacle that tries to come between us.

She rests her head against my shoulder, nuzzling into me in a way that makes me want to drag her home immediately instead of hanging out at this "party" to celebrate the resolution of the flurry of cases. "What time are you leaving tomorrow?"

I run my fingers through her hair. "A-a-after I've made s-s-sure you're thoroughly f-f-fucked and have e-e-eaten my favorite b-b-breakfast."

Her head jerks back, and I grin at her and waggle my eyebrows. She bursts out laughing, a flush spreading over her cheeks as she glances around to make sure no one heard my lewd comment. "You can't talk like that in public."

I raise a brow and scan the room. "L-l-like any of

these g-g-guys care and w-w-wouldn't say the same th-th-thing?"

Finley scowls at me, but there's no anger in it. "True." She releases a little sigh. "It's going to be weird—not seeing you every day."

I nod. "I kn-kn-know. B-b-but absence m-m-makes the heart g-g-grow fonder. Isn't th-th-that what they s-s-say?"

"I guess so." She flutters her lips against my ear, stirring my cock almost instantly. "You know, if we're going to do this long-distance thing, we're going to have to use the phone or Facetime or something and, you know, actually *talk*."

She pulls away and eyes me knowingly.

I scowl at her. "I s-s-see what you're d-d-doing."

"I would hope so since I'm being pretty blatant about it."

While it has gotten easier to talk to Finley without my ego and anxiety silencing me, around other people, it's a completely different story. She loves all the broken pieces of me, but that doesn't mean she won't keep trying to get me to move past some of them.

I press my lips to hers, which doesn't do anything for my straining erection, then move across her cheek to her ear. "D-d-do they have a ba-ba-bathroom in this place I can t-t-take you into to f-f-fuck you?"

Her eyes widen, and she slaps me playfully on the shoulder. "Stop it."

Before I can reiterate my intentions, Enzo approaches from across the bar and smiles at Finley. I'm man enough to admit when I'm jealous, and this smooth, handsome fucker makes me tighten my arm around her at my side possessively.

"Excuse me." Enzo clears his throat, shifting uncomfortably under my glare. "Ms. Banks, can I have a word?"

She glances at me briefly before pushing to her feet and following Enzo off to the side of the room to speak in private. I keep an eye on them, twisting my beer bottle in my hands when what I really want to do is smash it and use the pieces to remind him that she's mine.

Parrish approaches, his gaze darting from Finley to me, and he slides into the chair she just vacated.

I glare at him.

"Don't worry, fucker. I'm not staying long. She can have her seat back."

I snort and shake my head.

"I just wanted to say thanks again for all your help in getting the shitstorm that's been going on around here resolved. And for finally ending the Yankovich problem."

That final shot acted as a catharsis for all the anger and anguish I've held onto so tightly for so long. I completed the mission—and got the girl. So, while I may not like Parrish or the way he acted like I was his own personal mercenary, I still appreciate that if it weren't for him, I wouldn't have Finley.

I incline my head in acknowledgment of his thank you, and he slaps me on the shoulder and rises.

"I'm hoping I won't ever have to see any of you guys again. So, tell Reaper the same, but if you guys are ever in New York, you're always welcome here."

As annoyed as I am with how things have gone down since I got here, I appreciate the sentiment and offer him a nod of agreement.

"Back to the silent treatment, huh?"

I don't bother answering him, just return my focus to Enzo and Finley. The longer they stand together, talking, the more I want to walk over there, scoop her up, throw her over my shoulder like a damn caveman, and then bend her over the bar and bang her in front of everyone to prove who she belongs to.

All I can do is curl my hands into fists to keep myself from doing just that because he's a client and she *is* mine.

Forever.

She's helping me write my future on that cracked, broken slate, one that no one will be able to wipe away this time.

FINLEY

ENZO LEADS me over to the side of the room, as far as we can get from the raucous crowd of bikers and their women all over the bar.

He smiles sheepishly and glances at Jude, where he still sits at the table, glaring at us in a way that makes my lips twitch. "I just wanted to come over and thank you for all you did for me. I know I wasn't the easiest client."

I flash him a grin. "That's only because you had

trouble following directions when it came to our witness." My gaze drifts to the bar, where Danica waits for him, watching us closely. "It all worked out, though."

"Yeah"—he nods—"I guess it did."

Enzo was an absolute thorn in my side as a client—willfully violating the terms of his bond and potentially destroying our defense by being personally involved with the key witness—but considering the fact that I somehow fell in love with my *own* client, I really can't be too hard on him.

"You have my number, but I don't want you to ever have to use it again. You're a good guy, Enzo. It'd be a shame if you wound up being a pain-in-the-ass criminal like your old man."

At the mention of his father, Enzo's eyes dart around the room in search of Wolf. He sits at the end of the bar with Maria's arms wound around his neck, smiling back at his wife, relaxed and happier than I've ever seen him since Schwartz pulled me into this crazy world of the Satan's Knights.

Enzo shrugs with a laugh. "Eh, he's not that bad."

I snort and shake my head, about to argue that fact, when my gaze locks with Jude's where he sits with Parrish, looking like he's either going to strangle the man next to him or come over here and do it to Enzo.

Normally, a man's jealousy might annoy me and make me think he needs to work on his own self-esteem issues, but Jude's eyes blaze with so much heat that I actually squirm and press my legs together against the throb there.

Hell.

He's going to *prove* that I'm his—and it wouldn't surprise me if he's going to do it somewhere in this building where people are sure to walk by and either see and/or hear us.

As Parrish leaves his seat, I step away from Enzo and make my way back over to where Jude's waiting, but instead of sliding into my chair, I nudge him back from the table so I can sit on his lap.

His semi-hard cock presses against my ass, and I raise an eyebrow at him. "I thought you were just joking about doing me in the bathroom."

He shakes his head, grinning slightly, his hand moving up my exposed lower thigh and higher under the hem of my dress. "Oh, n-n-no. I n-n-never j-j-joke about anything like th-th-that."

I rest my head against his shoulder, squeezing my legs together to pin his hand and prevent it from going where he so clearly intends it to. "Were you jealous just now, seeing me talking to a former client?"

He stiffens under me slightly and shifts his weight, like he's uncomfortable with the question. I pull my head up and look at him.

"Not gonna answer me, huh?"

Jude remains stoic, not giving away anything, but it's all the answer I need.

"You know, I have to talk to other men to do my job, right? I can't just represent female clients because you're jealous."

Schwartz chuckles across the table.

Apparently, I didn't speak quietly enough.

My boss glances between Jude and me. "I mean, I guess I could assign you only female clients, and I could take all the men."

I glower at him. "Fuck you, Schwartz."

"You've already done that." His eyes dart over to Jude. "But now that you have this guy, I know it'll never happen again."

"About time you figured that out."

He turns away from us and rejoins his conversation with Charlotte, where she sits holding her new baby.

I wrap my arms around Jude's neck and snuggle into him, intentionally rubbing my ass against his cock to feel it grow harder under me.

"Wh-wh-what g-g-game are you p-p-playing, Finley?"

"No game. I'm just thinking it's time we get out of here."

He shakes his head. "No. H-h-here. N-n-now. I'm not w-w-waiting another s-s-second to get ins-s-side you."

Hell.

That growly, demanding man thing shouldn't be so hot, but it is. The fact that he's willing to tell me exactly what he wants and needs from me and isn't embarrassed by the way it comes out anymore warms my heart to match the heat spreading between my legs.

Jude climbs to his feet, letting me slide down until mine hit the sticky floor, then takes my hand in his and drags me past the dozens of people mingling in the bar to the side door that leads out to the patio.

The crisp early fall air hits the bare skin on my exposed legs, and Jude drags me under the tent erected over the old wooden deck and to the far corner—about as much privacy as we'll ever get around here with so many people milling about. It will only be a matter of minutes before someone stumbles out of the bar to have a smoke, so we're either going to have to accept that we will have an audience, or we're going to have to work fast.

Something tells me that isn't going to be a problem.

Jude is so tense and tightly wound that there isn't any way he intends this to be anything other than hard and fast. Which is fine by me. I'll take him any way he wants me, anytime. I want to spend every last minute I have here with him since it's going to be almost a week before I can head down to Baltimore to see him again.

It's going to feel like an eternity after being with him practically every day for a month, but it's time for him to go home, to return to the life he has there with his friends and his business.

He tugs me over to one of the rickety, old tables set up under the tent, grabs me by my hips, and lifts me easily, setting me on the top and instantly reaching for his waistband. The cold metal bites against my thighs, and he frees his hard cock and forces the skirt of my dress up around my waist, exposing me to him and the cold air—not to mention anyone who walks out after us.

That thought makes my pussy clench, and he uses the fingers of one hand to shove my thong to the side while the other strokes his length, pre-cum already beading at the large tip.

My mouth waters to suck him between my lips, but there isn't any time for that now. He lowers his head and kisses me deeply, dragging his cock through my wetness and slipping inside me easily. I gasp into his mouth, clinging to the back of his neck as he tugs my hips to the edge of the table to get even deeper.

"I w-w-want you to f-f-feel me inside y-y-you every f-f-fucking second th-th-this entire w-w-week while we're a-a-apart." He pulls his hips back, then sinks into me again, sending the table creaking and skittering slightly across the worn wood of the deck. "Every t-t-time y-y-you w-w-walk, I w-w-want you to f-f-feel my c-c-cock between your l-l-legs and remember that y-y-you're *mine.*"

"God, yes, Jude. Yours. All fucking yours."

Because I am his.

All his.

No matter what he does at night.

No matter who he was before.

I know who he is *now.*

He's the incredibly complicated man who knows how to reach a part of me I didn't know needed it. The one who made me see beyond my career to something else. The only one who will ever hold my heart.

Each drive of his hips cements our future even more. Each groan and grunt and moan of pleasure, the sounds of us committing to making *this* work, whatever it takes.

His thrusts become harsher, more erratic, and he jerks my head up to devour my mouth again as I squeeze around him and spur him to move faster with my hips meeting his. The grind of his pelvis against my clit finally sends me flying, lights flashing against my closed lids, my lips falling open on a strangled moan of release. He pumps into me relentlessly, chasing his own orgasm, and dips his head to dig his teeth into the soft flesh of my collarbone.

The bite of pain mixing with the ecstasy engulfing me drags out my bliss longer, and he empties himself into me on a groan and tightening of his hands at my hips.

Jude Lawson just marked me—in more ways than one.

I belong to him and his mouth, forever.

EPILOGUE

SIX MONTHS LATER

MOUTH

"Is this what normal looks like?" Chaos inclines his head toward where Viktoria, Avery, and Finley sit near the fire pit, laughing and sipping their margaritas.

The early spring weather is a welcome change from the snowy cold winter we've had. Being able to get out here and enjoy the outdoors allows us all to breathe some fresh air while we have a few drinks and some burgers thrown on Reaper's grill.

I shrug and glance at Reaper on the other side of me in our deck chairs. "I d-d-don't know. What do you th-th-think?"

He chuckles. "I mean, I guess it is." He spreads his arms wide, motioning to his yard, which hasn't quite come fully back to green after the long winter. "Just three normal guys barbecuing while their women gossip about God only knows what."

Only most guys didn't just come straight here from eliminating two men who robbed a liquor store, killed the clerk, and walked out of court scot-free...

I bark out a laugh and shake my head as I take a drink of my beer. "I c-c-can only imagine wh-wh-what those th-th-three are talking about."

Probably none of it good, considering how well those women know us and what loose lips they seem to have when they're together. It's incredible to see how quickly they've all bonded. Even with Finley only being able to come a couple times a month, they're three peas in a pod, like they've known each other their entire lives. Undoubtedly, Avery and Viktoria know far too much about our sex life and everything else that should stay just between Finley and me. But I suppose that's just the price you pay for having love in your life—from a good woman and good friends.

Chaos shifts in his seat, suddenly stiff and awkward when he's been so relaxed since we arrived. "So, guys..."

We both turn toward him, my gut churning slightly at the sudden shift to seriousness in his tone.

"Watch the girls and tell me if you notice anything unusual."

I narrow my focus on them, trying to see what he does that has him so concerned. The last thing we need after so many months of relatively uneventful life is for another major drama to come up—especially when this is one of my weekends with Finley. I don't want to be distracted by anything else so I can concentrate on spending every waking moment with her.

Viktoria, Avery, and Finley whisper conspiratorially, occasionally glancing our way as they try to pour Avery's drink into their glasses.

I jerk my head toward Chaos. "I-i-is she pr-pr-pregnant?"

He grins and nods, and Reaper leaps from his chair and pulls Chaos off his, embracing him and clapping him on the back.

"Holy shit, man! That's amazing."

Lumbering to my feet, I offer him a hug. "C-c-congratulations. You guys d-d-deserve it."

"Did they just figure it out?" Avery yells across the yard, giggling.

Chaos nods to her. "Yep, took them long enough."

Avery rolls her eyes and laughs. "And I thought you guys were supposed to be super observant."

We burst out laughing as the women all climb to their feet and make their way over toward us, smug looks on all their faces.

Viktoria appears incredibly pleased with herself. "I told you these assholes wouldn't notice. It took my keen cop eye, which none of them have."

"Hey, I f-f-figured it out."

Finley slides next to me and tucks herself under my arm, staring up at me with a grin. "Yeah, but I knew the minute we got here and I saw her. She's practically glowing."

I shrug. "H-h-how the h-h-hell am I supposed to kn-kn-know what a pregnant w-w-woman looks like?"

Something flashes in Finley's eyes that makes the blood rush straight to my cock.

Fuck.

I dip my head down to brush my lips over her ear. "H-h-how about we f-f-find somewhere inside for me to t-t-try to put one in y-y-you?"

She jerks her head back, her mouth opening and closing a few times before she finally manages to speak. Finley is usually the last one at a loss for words, but I've managed to render her speechless. "Yeah..."

"Yeah?" I raise an eyebrow at her, laughing at the stunned look still on her face.

Even though it's only been six months, and we haven't ever really talked about it, the thought of seeing her belly growing with my baby inside it, of being a father, just feels right. Like that's what's meant to happen and what all the turmoil we've been through has all been about.

"E-e-excuse me, g-g-guys. Finley n-n-needs to show me so-so-something in the h-h-house."

They all give us smug, knowing looks as I grab her hand and drag her toward the two-story bungalow Reaper and Viktoria bought on the outskirts of Baltimore.

We step in through the back door, and Finley releases a giggle, squeezing my hand.

"Are we really doing this?"

I lead her into the downstairs bathroom and push

her up against the door. "Y-y-you telling me you r-r-really want a baby with m-m-me?"

Uncertainty flashes in her gaze. "I don't know. Jude, it's only been six months."

"The ha-ha-happiest six m-m-months of my l-l-life. My n-n-new one. The o-o-one that is my f-f-future, n-n-not about the p-p-past. I w-w-want to fill my h-h-head with all n-n-new memories, w-w-with you at the c-c-center of all of th-th-them."

Her expression softens, and she presses her palms against my face. "I love you so much."

"I l-l-love you, t-t-too. N-n-now, about p-p-putting that b-b-baby inside you."

She giggles, her head falling back, exposing her neck, almost in offering. I lean in and kiss her there, and she fumbles with the button and zipper on my jeans to finally free my cock.

It wasn't really an answer to my question, but we've come to the point where we don't even need words. Ironic since I'm finally becoming more comfortable with actually talking again.

I slip a hand down under the hem of her dress, expecting to find something blocking my path, but my fingers only brush against moisture already covering her pussy.

"N-n-no panties?"

She grins and shakes her head. "When I'm down here visiting you, I much prefer the easiest access possible. If we're only going to see each other a few days a month, we need to make good use of them." Something twinkles in her eyes that makes my cock jerk. "Especially with this new goal in mind."

Fuck yes.

I never thought I'd be the guy who gets off on thinking about knocking up his woman, but I don't think I've ever wanted to be inside her more than I do at this very second. "I c-c-couldn't agree m-m-more."

FINLEY

Our new goal.

A baby.

A tiny version of Jude walking around with my attitude and his father's big heart.

It's crazy.

It's far too much, far too fast.

We shouldn't even be considering this when we haven't discussed it. When I'm still living in New York and he's down here. When we've only been seeing each other a few days every month when my schedule allows me to come down or his missions give him time to come to New York.

A baby?

Anyone who saw us would say we're crazy, that we're just caught up in the joy of Avery and Chaos' moment, that we're just horny for each other because of the time we spend apart and that all of this will come crashing down around us violently when we take time to consider what we're doing.

Jude and I have a history of making rash decisions and jumping into things without looking, yet, the moment he said those words to me, it just sounded... right. Just like everything with him has felt once I worked past my own guilt over us hooking up while I was representing him.

Jude drags the head of his cock through my wetness and sinks inside me in one long stroke that feels like coming home.

Every time we're together, all the stress of work and traveling back and forth disappears and it's like we've never been apart. I cling to his neck, and we move together fluidly, knowing each other so well, knowing exactly what the other likes and needs, like pieces of a puzzle fitting together, completing a perfect picture that was always meant to be.

A picture in my mind that suddenly has more than just the two of us in it.

All this talk about making a baby has me hotter for him than I've ever been, my blood burning like fire through my veins, rushing to all the places he touches me—desperate for something I never knew I wanted.

A family.

A man worshipping me.

I always thought my career was my partner, that no one would ever understand the amount of time I have to work, the amount of stress I have, the weight that holding the lives of my clients in my hands puts on me.

But Jude gets it. He gets me. He understands exactly what I need in the bedroom and everywhere else, and he'll do anything to give it to me.

He drags back his hips and plunges into me again, then pulls us away from the door and turns to set me on the counter, placing me at the perfect height to pound into me relentlessly.

His hands at my waist keep me from slamming against the mirror behind me with his aggressive thrusts, and I roll my hips up to meet each one, rocking against him and digging my nails into his nape.

With one violent tug, he moves me closer to the edge so he can pump deeper, push harder, force himself all the way into me. I drop my head back on a moan, every cell in my body heating and exploding with the pleasure he always brings me. That sense of rightness that's always there.

One of his large, calloused palms finds my cheek and tilts my face to his. He crushes his lips to mine, kissing me with the same passion and need as he did that first night when I wasn't willing to give in, wasn't willing to admit that I was incapable of resisting what was happening between us.

Everything I risked was worth it for this moment.

We have a future full of friends and happiness and the knowledge that everything's going to work out. If Jude could make it through everything he's had to face to get here, then nothing can stand in our way.

I return his kiss, with every ounce of love I hold for

him, and grind on his cock, squeezing him the way I know makes him insane.

It doesn't matter that the others know exactly what we're doing in here or that they can probably hear us.

I don't care.

Let them hear me scream.

Let them hear exactly what this man does to me.

I couldn't care less.

Jude reaches between us and finds my clit, rolling his thumb over it expertly, and I come like a freight train barreling down the tracks, unable to stop. It slams into me, drawing out a gasp as he holds me steady and pounds into me, a man on a mission—apparently to knock me up.

His other work might raise some lingering questions, but this is a mission I am fully on board with. One I'm more than willing to let him succeed in because Mouth is my future, and I'm his new reality.

He finally comes on a groan, somehow plunging impossibly deeper into me, and he stills with his face buried against my neck.

We remain like this panting for a few moments, our hearts thundering against each other before he finally lifts his head and takes my face between his palms. "J-j-just seeing y-y-you on the w-w-weekends isn't enough."

"I know. I've been thinking about it for a while, and I'll move down here. I'll take the bar in Maryland, and I can still take a few cases in New York if I want to. I have to stay until Schwartz's suspension is over to handle things at the office. But then, I'm coming back here to you forever."

The scars and ruins of his past have made Jude what he is today. He might be broken and battered by what happened to him, by what he's suffered, and those wounds may never heal. But even if it means spending the rest of our lives working for it, one day, he's going to find his voice again and won't be afraid to tell other people how he feels about them the way he does with me.

One day soon.

———

I hope you enjoyed the Scarred Heroes Series. Want more from the Sins of the Mafia World?

Grab the Sins of the Mafia Collections here: https:// books2read.com/rl/SinsoftheMafiaWorld

Sign up for Gwyn's newsletter to stay up to date on releases and other news: www.gwynmcnamee.com/ newsletter

ABOUT THE AUTHOR

Gwyn McNamee is an attorney, writer, wife, and mother (to one human baby and two fur babies). Originally from the Midwest, Gwyn relocated to her husband's home town of Las Vegas in 2015 and is enjoying her respite from the cold and snow. Gwyn has been writing down her crazy stories and ideas for years and finally decided to share them with the world. She loves to write stories with a bit of suspense and action mingled with romance and heat.

When she isn't either writing or voraciously devouring any books she can get her hands on, Gwyn is busy adding to her tattoo collection, golfing, and stirring up trouble with her perfect mix of sweetness and sarcasm (usually while wearing heels).

Gwyn loves to hear from her readers.
Here is where you can find her:
NewsletteR:
www.gwynmcnamee.com/newsletter
Facebook:
https://www.facebook.com/AuthorGwynMcNamee/
Twitter:
https://twitter.com/GwynMcNamee

Instagram:

https://www.instagram.com/gwynmcnamee

Bookbub:

https://www.bookbub.com/authors/gwyn-mcnamee

FB Reader Group:

https://www.facebook.com/groups/1667380963540655/

Website:

https://www.gwynmcnamee.com